THE ENVOYS IN THE MULTIVERSE

ONE

THE DISCOVERY OF THE VINE

TAYLOR SORENSEN

innovo
PUBLISHING

Published by Innovo Publishing, LLC
www.innovopublishing.com
1-888-546-2111

Providing Full-Service Publishing Services for Christian Authors, Artists &
Ministries: Books, eBooks, Audiobooks, Music, Screenplays, Film & Curricula

THE DISCOVERY OF THE VINE
Volume 1 in The Envoys in the Multiverse Series

Library of Congress Control Number: 2022911168
ISBN: 978-1-61314-856-3

Cover Design & Interior Layout: Innovo Publishing, LLC

Printed in the United States of America
U.S. Printing History
First Edition: 2022

ACKNOWLEDGMENTS

None of this would be possible without You, God. Thank You for growing me in Your truth, for being patient with me when I fail, and for giving me the grace to overcome. May this book bring You glory and mightily advance Your kingdom!

I also want to thank you, Mom and Dad, for loving God enough to honor Him in everything and loving me enough to show me Christ and all He's done. Thank you for discipling me in the fun and hard times so that I might know more and more about our Father. Thanks also to my four younger brothers, Brett, Scott, Todd, and Jack, for always keeping things fun! It's always been a blast making up stories with you guys.

I also want to thank my cousin, Leanna Jackson. You sparked this whole idea of a fictitious multiverse with a simple *what if* question. Much of the inspiration came from you.

I want to give a big thanks to my friends and leaders at my church, First Southern Baptist in Del City. You have taught me more about the real Jesus and the real mission in just a couple of years than I had ever known. Thank you for showing me what the church is meant to be!

Finally, thank you, Rachael Carrington, my editor and project manager. You have made a very complicated process simple and stress free for me, and your prompt, personal, and encouraging interactions with me are so appreciated.

"Yes, I am the vine; you are the branches. Those who remain in me, and I in them, will produce much fruit. For apart from me you can do nothing."

—*John 15:5*

PROLOGUE

C *lang! Clang!* The bright orange metal changed shape slightly with every blow. Between the mighty, rectangular hammer and the dark anvil, the steel began to take the form of a fearsome mace. The head, a ball where several spikes would be placed, was perfectly rounded. It had a small rod sticking out where the handle would be fashioned. The spikes, each shaped and vaguely sharpened earlier, sat at a nearby table, waiting to be quenched and assembled.

The forger of this remarkable weapon was a strong and formidable being. He was about seven feet tall and had black hair down to his shoulders. He had two pairs of wings, two for flying, two for armor. He was very focused on his work, and nothing could distract him. He took the now cool, red steel and placed it into an oven quite larger than the typical size. Once the mace was scalding again, he grabbed it with a pair of black tongs and dipped it into a vat of oil. Flames spouted from the surface. The weapon itself was spewing fire and smoke when it was freed from the oil. One swift breath from the forger, and the flames disappeared. He did this with each of the spikes as well.

Once everything was quenched and dried, the smith sharpened the spikes fully, attached each of them to the head, and polished it all. He looked at the weapon and said in a deep grunt, "The work is complete."

The forger then put the mace on a shelf with dozens of other unique weapons. Afterward, he took a sizeable block of steel and began to forge a new weapon. This time, an axe.

Clang! Clang! Clang!

A while later, the two large axe heads on either side of the bar, which would be inserted into a strong, wooden shaft, could be clearly seen now. The spike at the end came to the desirable length. For one last time, he placed the glowing red axe in the furnace. He was just about to submerge the work in the oil when two strange creatures entered his forge.

These strangers arrived through a shining white portal with a green border. The white inside it was so bright that it was impossible to see to the other side. One of the two beings was a faun with chrome armor, and the other was an elf with black armor. The forger stood still near the furnace and the now smoldering axe. He was rather surprised by this visit, even more so than usual.

"Lisias," he said, acknowledging the faun, "what brings you here? I haven't seen you in ages. I thought you had forsaken the Vine for good."

Lisias said, "O Azarias, forger and keeper of this realm, *Chârâsh*, the forge of the Envoys of the Great Vine, I greet you humbly. I had a change of heart. This is my friend, Ives. The Great Vine Nazir sent us to acquire something from you."

"Oh?" Azarias said. "For greeting me humbly, you used the vocabulary of a very self-esteemed person. What might that something be?"

"The Sword of *Chârâsh*, the teleportation sword."

"What?!" said the forger. "The Sword of *Chârâsh* is the most valuable item here, other than myself! Why would Nazir let you and your friend, who is not an Envoy of his because he does not wear the badge like you do, have such a treasure?"

"Yes," said Lisias, "these facts are total truth, yet Nazir still wants you to give it to me. He's called us to a critical mission. Desperate times call for desperate measures."

"You forget that the Great Vine holds the power of all treasures such as the Sword," said Azarias, "and he doesn't want just anyone wielding it. Also, he is not so desperate that he calls someone who is not redeemed by him—in this case, this Ives—to a mission so exclusively for Envoys. He does use non-Envoys, but not like this."

At this point, the winged creature could see what was to come. He would not prevent it. His hand slowly crept toward the axe, which was still in the oven. The pair of visitors began to circle him. They were focused on him, though their eyes darted to and fro, searching for the special Sword.

"You haven't turned back to the Envoys!" said the forger. "You want the Sword for your own plans, not Nazir's!"

"Choose your last words wisely, fiend," said Lisias, placing his hand on the handle of his own mortal, sheathed sword.

Azarias swiftly swung the slightly deformed, beaming white axe out of the fire. "Leave now, before there is violence."

The faun suddenly lunged at the forger, his blade waving furiously. "Find the Sword, Ives!"

As Azarias deflected his opponent's attack, his hair turned to fire, showing the mighty forger's fury and zeal. This always happened when he battled. It served to surprise and intimidate his opponents, though the faun had seen him fight before.

Lisias had quite a bit of fighting experience, but Azarias easily bested him. He kicked the faun into a distant shelf, then swung the hot axe at Ives, who was not completely prepared. He got a burning scar on his arm (though it was not severed), and his armor was toast—quite literally. Before the elf could be killed, Lisias attacked the forger from behind and almost took the creature's head off, if not for his wings, which batted the faun away.

Lisias and Azarias fought for another minute or so before Ives recovered. The elf, unarmed, jumped directly behind the defender, between the wings so they could not swat him off, and began to choke Azarias out. The forger dropped to his knees beside the anvil, gasping for any amount of air, trying to use his free hand to break the choke.

Finally, he saw the large mallet on the anvil and grabbed it. Before Ives could leap away, the forger smacked him on his helmet's side. Ives would have a headache for days after that.

Azarias, catching a second wind, flew up and beat on his opponents with both the hammer and the axe. It was not long after that that the two invaders fled, their mission having failed. Lisias, with a new, hot scar across his face, grabbed a green Dagger from his belt and from it shot a green ray into thin air, making a new portal. They sprinted through and disappeared with the portal but not before Azarias heard Ives say, "Maybe we could take the elven world without it."

"Good luck," mumbled the victorious forger, whose fiery hair had cooled and returned to normal. "The Vine would never let them through."

Azarias looked around the now cluttered and untidy forge. He then glanced at the cold, red weapon in his hand and said to himself, *I should probably scrap this piece.*

PART I

A NEW DAY

1
LEGENDS TO BE

S tonesboro was not a spectacular place, considering it was
in a spectacular universe. One might find it as a suburb of
Craghill, a city on Virginia's northern coast. Craghill smelled
of the sea, which could be seen on its rocky shore, while
Stonesboro smelled of bricks and exhaust. Craghill shone just as
brightly as any medium-sized city, while Stonesboro was much
smaller and harder to find amongst Craghill's complexity.

In one of the rougher neighborhoods in Stonesboro lived
a woman named Leona Ferris. She lived near her mother who
loved her and always did what was best. Sometimes, though,
Leona did not think this was true. Leona had thick, intricate
braids (some of which were dyed red) down to her shoulders.
She had green eyes and was very fit. She also was short for her
twenty-two-year age. Because of this, she was often the target of
sneering and even physical bullying at the college she attended.
After a few months of training at a judo school, she learned to
fight back in a justified way. She never retorted when someone
verbally made fun of her, but if she sensed real danger, she would
extinguish it. She was warned once by the principal not to hurt
anyone again. This was wrong on the principal's part, as Leona
was defending herself from physical danger. Nevertheless, Leona
never needed to defend herself from those bullies again.

In the larger city of Craghill, there lived a very successful family named the Brandts. They lived in an uncommonly large house complete with a pool, fountains, and hedges, plus basketball and tennis courts. The Brandts had two sons: Ambrose and Dilyn. Ambrose had sleek, blond hair that was spiked at the top and had buzz cuts on the sides. He had blue eyes and a thin moustache. Ambrose had the potential to be just as successful as his parents. He was intelligent and remarkably athletic. There was a good chance that he would go to Yale after finishing high school, or he would become a superstar athlete, or even both! This caused a problem with arrogance because he knew this all too well.

Dilyn was Ambrose's younger brother. He had rich, red, combed hair and a round face with blue eyes. He had a tall and skinny build but was healthy. Dilyn, like many little brothers, preferred to follow his big brother in every way. He was not as athletic, but he was just as intelligent—if not more so—than Ambrose, but he still liked to rely on his brother's judgement. His friends, who were also Ambrose's friends, all told Dilyn to be himself and to branch out and be independent, but his refusal was shown by his actions.

Both brothers went to the same high school, which was associated with the college Leona was attending. Ambrose and Dilyn all earned exceptional grades, and their teachers and parents were very proud of them. Meanwhile, Leona tended to struggle with learning, even with the professors' exclusive help. Leona and Ambrose were both seniors, while Dilyn was a freshman. That's what they were when came the first of many fateful days.

On that day, the school board decided to put together a summer field trip to Philadelphia after school ended. Ambrose and Dilyn signed up as soon as they heard (with their parents' approval, of course). Leona wanted to go, since they allowed college students to be assistant leaders, but it was enough of a financial stretch for her mom to afford putting her in such a good school. A field trip to a distant city seemed out of the question. Unexpectedly and by no small coincidence, Ms. Ferris got an email saying one of the other leaders dropped out from the trip, and since it was already paid for, Leona could be the replacement. It seemed a bit strange to Leona that the other person did not want his money back, but she was elated by her sudden ability to go.

Soon, school was over. Ambrose graduated high school as valedictorian, and Dilyn finished his freshman year. Leona also got her bachelor's degree. Even though she just barely made it with a 3.0 GPA, she earned it and was proud of her achievement.

The day for the trip arrived. On a fair Friday morning in May, Leona, Dilyn, Ambrose, and thirty other high school and college students embarked on a school bus bound for Philadelphia. Leona got in her seat, which was a few rows in front of and a column to the right from the Brandts. The brothers had attracted a large group of friends over the years, and they chatted and raved about the newest games and trends on their phones, all of which the Brandts seemed to have. For this and a number of additional reasons, Leona wondered how many real friends they actually had.

They finally arrived in Philadelphia after four hours. They first went to their hotel and unpacked their luggage. Once this was done, they reboarded the bus to go to a seafood restaurant. The ride for the first portion of the journey was clamorous. It seemed everyone, save the driver, was chatting. Leona herself was not without friends, and she found one or two with whom to pass the time.

About halfway to the destination, the bus driver stopped at a gas station to refuel. The leaders allowed the students to get off and stretch their legs. The students decided to stand on a curb near the street to observe the cars, drivers, and pedestrians. Two such pedestrians stopped to inquire what was happening.

These two, a man and a woman, seemed to be in the same age range as the other leaders; they were new seniors in college. The man had a thin, black crewcut and was on the skinnier side. The woman had brown hair arranged in a long ponytail, dark green eyes, and a slender build. With the backpacks and clothing, one could conclude that they were walking home from a summer class.

"What's going on?" said the woman. "I haven't seen this much of a racket since school ended."

"We're on a field trip from Virginia to see what it's like here in Philadelphia," said one of the students.

"I see," the woman said.

"Now that you mention it," said Ambrose, "what is Philly like in your perspective?"

"Oh, the same as any large city, I guess," said the man. "Busy and loud."

"So there's nothing special to see?" Ambrose said.

"Oh no, of course there is!" said the man. "There's the Independence Hall, the Liberty Bell, and many other sights."

"But you said it was the same as every city. Not every city in America has a big, cracked bell."

"He meant that every city is the same *in that* they're busy and loud," the woman said.

This argument went on for a while, and the tones and words uttered became angrier and angrier. Ambrose, his friends, and the couple had attracted the whole group of students who wanted to see what Ambrose would do next.

Finally, the field trip leaders announced that the bus was refueled, and the students should reembark. The leaders did not know what the argument was about, nor did they know with whom they were even arguing. They never would, as everyone left for the bus—except Leona. She, being quite reserved but not entirely shy, watched the whole verbal brawl from a distance. When the students were called, the pair started off down their original path. Ignoring the urgency to get back on board, she strode toward the duo and caught their attention.

"Hey," she said, "wait up."

They both turned to her. "You're with them, I'm assuming?" asked the man.

"If you mean I'm with the field trip group, then yes. If you mean I'm in the Brandts' friend group, I'll have to say no."

"So the young, arguing brats are the Brandts, huh?" the woman asked.

"Ambrose and Dilyn. They come from a very wealthy family."

"Oh," they both uttered in a way that meant they understood the wealthy people's type, but not firsthand.

"I'm Leona, by the way."

"My name is Bernice," said the woman, "and this is my friend, Amory."

Amory shook Leona's hand, as did Bernice.

"Do you two live here in Philadelphia?"

"You would think we do after our prior conversation with *them*," Amory said, "but I actually don't. Bernice does, but I live in a small house in a forest near her place."

"I see," said Leona, contemplating something. "Hey! My group is going on a tour of some old museums in the morning, and we're taking a break that afternoon. Why don't I come and hang out with you? I mean, unless you're busy or something."

Bernice's face unexpectedly lit up. "No, I actually like that idea! We don't have school or work tomorrow, and we're free all day."

"We're practically strangers to you," said Amory. "Why would you give up a field trip to hang out with us?"

"Well, for one thing, I need some more excitement. For another, you guys seem different from the people I've lived with my whole life. I don't know if it's big-city people versus smaller-town ones or what, but I want to get to know you better."

"All right," Amory said. "You can come to my house outside of town, and I can show you around the property. It's been in my family for generations. It's really quite amazing!"

"That sounds like fun!" Leona said. "Tomorrow at 1:30, then?"

"Yeah, that'll work! Where can we meet?" asked Bernice.

"We'll be staying at the Eagle Hotel," Leona said. "We can meet on that street or somewhere around there."

"It's a deal," Bernice said.

After being called severely by the main leader, Leona finally returned to the bus, and her new friends started off again toward their homes, a spring in both of their steps.

"That was interesting," said Bernice. "That's never happened before. I mean, a stranger wanting to hang out with us!"

"Perhaps it's best that she remains a stranger and doesn't know everything about us," chuckled Amory. "We wouldn't want to scare her away!"

"Oh, come on," Bernice replied with a grin. "We're not terrible people to hang out with. It's just that no one has ever wanted to before." They walked on a couple of blocks before Bernice continued, "Are you sure you want to meet at *your* house? What if she asks where your parents are, since you said it's your family's?"

"I've got that figured out. Don't worry."

"You're not going to tell her the truth though, are you? You're willing to tell a stranger that your parents—"

"*No*," Amory almost shouted, "I'm not going to tell her that, but I'm not going to outright lie either. I'll just say that they're away, that's all." There were a few more minutes spent in silence. "Did I ever thank you for helping me all throughout school after *that* happened?"

"Only about a million times," smiled Bernice.

"Seriously, though. I was left to raise myself, and I was utterly alone. No one else was comfortable enough to hang around me. But you were willing to go beyond your typical lifestyle to advise, guide, and assist me whenever I needed it. I know it's been about a decade since then, but I'm still very grateful and even indebted to you!"

"You don't owe me a thing, Amory. If you want to do something for me, let's have fun tomorrow! Well, here's my street. Thanks for walking with me." Bernice started to cross the road. "I have to hurry and eat and then get to work. A waitress's work is never done!"

"Bernice," called Amory, getting her to turn before she crossed, "I've got the strangest feeling about this whole idea of meeting with this Leona girl. It's not a bad feeling, just an eerie one. It's like when that one anonymous person paid for the rest of my school fees after *that* happened. It feels like there's something bigger going on, or like someone is controlling it all. I don't know, but I just had to voice it."

"I feel the same thing," said Bernice. "I don't know why, but I'm starting to really look forward to this! See you then!"

This was the only indication that there would be any adventure at all, but little did the three of them know what their next adventure would bring and how much their lives would change. In fact, almost no part of their lives now would eventually stay the same. But they weren't worried about that right then. Leona was just focused on getting back to the hotel, and Amory and Bernice were focused on getting home, all in time for dinner, which was sandwiches for some and burgers for others.

2

INSIDE THE CAVERN

The next sunrise came—the second fateful day—and Leona went with her group to take tours of Philadelphia's several museums. She marveled at the artifacts and displays, but her mind remained on her two new companions and the unknown adventures that would lie within that afternoon. They had visited two galleries before going to lunch and heading back to the hotel.

Leona neatly arranged her things in her part of the room and put her favorite purple hoodie over her yellow and gray outfit to prepare for a potential storm, but that storm would never come. She then quietly left the room. She went into the elevator and waited patiently for the large metallic doors to close.

I'm glad I'm going down alone, she thought. *Then no one will suspect a thing.* For she was quite reserved, and it would take a great deal of time before anyone noticed she was missing.

The doors were almost shut when a burly hand shot through the gap and caused the doors to reopen. Leona groaned internally. On the other side of the doors stood Ambrose and Dilyn, both in red, expensive-looking sweatshirts. They looked curiously at her.

"Where are you going?" Ambrose asked as they walked in.

"I might ask you the same thing," Leona replied.

"We're going to ask about the Wi-Fi password downstairs."

"You didn't do it last night?"

"We forgot. Your turn."

". . . I'm going to get a snack from the vending machine," said Leona.

"We just had lunch."

"Didn't fill me up."

At that point, the elevator had reached the first floor, and they got out.

"Make sure to come right back," Ambrose said. "The leaders don't want us wandering around."

"You do the same," Leona said, wanting him to remember who of them was the adult.

The two brothers went around a corner and stopped. Ambrose turned to watch Leona, disbelieving everything she had told them. Dilyn followed suit. Keeping out of sight, they observed as she walked straight to the vending machine.

Hiddenly desperate to find some money in her pockets, she finally found enough for a bag of corn chips. After retrieving it from the awkward slot, she stood up, looked around, and headed for the door. As soon as she left, Ambrose started after her.

"Wait," whispered Dilyn, putting a hand on his brother's arm, which seemed to annoy Ambrose very much. "The leaders did say not to leave the hotel. We'll get in trouble if they find we've been gone."

Ambrose rolled his eyes. "And if we do, we'll tell them we were following Leona to get her to come back, and the blame will be on her. And she's one of the leaders. She's a hypocrite if she does something she told us not to do."

"I still think it's disrespectful to trail a leader. She probably has a good reason for leaving. What gives you the right to know?"

Ambrose's reply came in his angry, yet smirking expression.

"Is that what we're doing?" Dilyn continued. "I mean, getting her to come back?"

"That depends."

"On what?" asked Dilyn.

"On where she's going."

———

Leona came to the end of the block before spotting Bernice and Amory at a lamppost. They greeted each other, then climbed into Amory's truck, which was rather clean considering Amory was in college. The Brandt brothers snuck into the truck's bed before it drove off, unbeknownst to those in the cab. They traveled out of the city and down a country road through the woods.

"So are you two dating?" asked Leona from the back seat.

"No, not yet," said Amory in almost a sigh. "Not until I'm readier and more responsible."

"I think he is already, but he persistently disagrees. We probably will soon, though," said Bernice.

Suddenly they drove over a shallow pothole and heard a large thump behind them. They turned to find Ambrose and Dilyn in the trunk, desperately trying to hold onto anything. Amory immediately stopped the truck, and the trio stepped out.

"What the heck are you doing?!" Leona asked.

"I might ask you the same thing," Ambrose said, mimicking Leona's tone when she had made the same reply earlier.

Seeing that lying would no longer do any good, she said, "I'm spending time with my new friends. What, you don't have friends of your own to hang out with?"

Ambrose grinned at the remark. "Where are you headed?"

"To my home," said Amory. "Leona said she had some free time, and we thought we might hang there."

"Must be some house," said Ambrose, not taking his gaze off Leona, "if it's worth breaking the rules set by the other field trip leaders."

Bernice, who seemed to be the only one keeping her cool, proposed a resolution. "Why don't you come with us and see for yourself?"

Bernice knew she got a dirty look from Amory, but she didn't look at him. She peaceably invited the brothers into the cab and convinced Amory to drive on. Bernice knew the Brandts would like the house if they had the taste they seemed to have. She was right. As the house came into view, she watched as their faces showed low expectations being greatly exceeded.

Amory's home was a short, two-story colonial stone cottage reinforced at the corners with thick mahogany posts. The roof, complete with a stone chimney, was made with old-fashioned but strong gray shingles. The cottage's fantastical charm was perfected by its wooded environment.

They went inside and were even more impressed. The classic wooden furniture, the stone fireplace, and the inexpensive but nonetheless delightful paintings all contributed to its enthrallment. As they walked into the living room, Ambrose spoke.

"This is quite the place you've got here, sir. What was your name?"

"Amory Walters," he said, extending a hand. "This is Bernice Banner. And you are?"

"Ambrose Brandt," he said, firmly shaking the hand given. "And that's my brother, Dilyn."

Amory already knew their names but was polite to ask anyway. Handshakes were exchanged all around, with the exception of Leona, who already knew everyone present.

"Where are your parents, Amory?" Leona asked.

"Uh, they're on a business trip," he said, stealing a glance at Bernice, who made a conspicuous face.

"They must do very well for themselves."

"Yes . . . they do. Being a mechanic's apprentice helps too."

"So you're taking care of yourself while they're gone?" asked Dilyn.

"Yup. Would any of you like a snack or drink? I have water, milk, iced tea, coffee, soda, cookies, bananas, apples. . . ."

"No, thanks," said Leona, taking out her bag of cool ranch flavored triangles. "I got something."

Ambrose took a red delicious apple and some water (he had to stay fit for football and school), while Amory just had tea, and the rest had oatmeal cookies and cold milk.

"I hope your parents don't mind us eating their food," Dilyn said.

"They never do," said Amory. "I thought after we eat, we could go exploring around the property."

"How much property do you have?" asked Ambrose.

"About fifty acres of pure forest. Some of it even I haven't explored yet!"

"Let's do it!" said Bernice, shoving in the rest of her cookie.

They all headed out the back door and started off for the woods, Amory leading.

"Hey," Ambrose said, "why isn't your house fenced in? Not exactly the best safety precaution, you know."

"The entire estate is fenced in instead of just the house," said Amory. "That way there's an even lesser chance of anything being harmed."

"I see," Ambrose said.

Amory led them due north for a time until he came to the place he had stopped and gone back the last time he'd explored. From that point on, they simply went where there was no excess of thorns or any other danger. As they looked about them, they were in awe of the trees' gorgeousness. Rays of gilded sunlight peered through the leaves, which sprouted from fine, thick branches reaching from strong trunks armored in brown bark.

The plants on the ground and on the trees were just as stunning. Flowers of numerous colors were seen in all directions. Bright green moss grew from the trunks and were soft to the touch. There were bushes, some green, others red. Some bore poisonous fruit, some bore delightful berries to which the explorers helped themselves, and others bore none at all. There were also vines—lots of vines. In fact, the further along they went, the more vines grew. After a few minutes of it, they started to take notice.

"These wouldn't happen to be poisonous, would they?" Leona asked.

"I don't know," Amory said back. "Why, did you touch one?"

"No, just making sure."

They trudged on. None of them realized that they had been walking on a stone floor since Leona had spoken up, at least until Dilyn suddenly put his foot through a weak spot. They all instantly looked back at him and listened as the large stone that had given way crashed below them a second after he had stepped through it. It was then that they saw their man-made terrain.

"Uh, did you know this was here?" Bernice asked, her voice a tad shaky.

"N-o," said Amory, his voice even shakier.

"Let's go into it!" Ambrose said, looking inside the newly discovered cavern. "Maybe we'll find a hidden treasure and become rich!"

"I thought you already were," said Leona.

Ambrose squinted at her in a very harsh way.

Leona looked at her watch. She had been keeping track of time to make sure they weren't staying away from the field trip group too long.

"It's 3:00," she said. "They'll have started another tour by now, and they'll be wondering where we are, especially with the Brandts missing."

"Nah, I think we have a little time left to see what's inside."

"Probably venomous spiders and deadly traps," said Bernice, who was the least keen about going down. "Just like in all those treasure-hunting movies and books."

Bernice couldn't convince them. Neither could Leona. They all gathered around the hole, trying to see how far down it went. The angle of the sun did not help them; it fell almost to the tall trees' heights.

"The stone landed only a second after it came off," said Dilyn. "I think it'll be OK. If we fall, it won't be far."

"Who wants to go first?" asked Ambrose, looking at the two ladies present. Bernice glared at him, but Leona shrugged it off.

"I'll go," she said, even with some enthusiasm.

Amory got beside Ambrose and helped her down by hanging on to her hands and lowering her. She felt for the floor with her feet but touched nothing. She looked around and saw only cold, damp, vine-ridden walls with black in between them. She looked down. Her eyes had adjusted to the darkness, and she saw a bit of floor less than two feet below her.

"The floor's close enough," she said. "Just drop me."

They did.

Leona landed safely on her feet, but she stood perfectly still, except for moving her head to make sure she was clear of any potential traps. Finally she gave her friends a thumbs up, and they climbed down one-by-one. First Dilyn, then Bernice (with a little persuading), Amory, and then Ambrose, who simply jumped in.

"Anyone have any flashlights?" Leona asked, just as Ambrose came down. The unanimous answer was no.

"Seriously?" asked Bernice, who now was losing her patience. "We went into a really strange cave without thinking about what *might* be needed?"

"I guess we'll just have to walk in the dark," said Ambrose, who didn't really care about any dangers.

"We can't do that!" Amory said. "What if there *are* traps in here?"

Ambrose ignored him. He took one step forward, then another, then another, until the others couldn't see him.

"See," he called back, "I'm fine."

Just then, he stopped. He heard something like a big crackle. The others heard it too, and they waited in silence to be spontaneously, violently killed. Instead, they saw a fire start on the walls. The flames continued in both directions.

"Great," said Bernice, "Ambrose set the walls on fire."

Amory looked closer at where the fire was coming from. He discovered that each wall had a hollow extension that contained oil, like a long, continuous sink, and that they were meant to light the path.

"Onward," he said after explaining this. "Now we can see where we're going."

So on they went. They followed the path Ambrose had originally taken until they came to a dead end. As soon as they saw this, they turned back and tried a different way. Had they gone all the way to that last wall, the floor would have given way, and they would have fallen into a seemingly endless pit.

There were many doomful ends to several paths they took. There were spikes, quicksand, boulders, and as many other dangers as you can imagine. They each had careful eyes, however, and were able to evade every trap without even setting them off. By now, their hoodies were either wrapped around their waists or carried over their shoulders, as it was rather humid. They tried a couple dozen ways, all of which came to dead ends. Finally they decided to go back to their entrance. There was, however, one problem: they couldn't find it. They had gotten lost.

Amory, Dilyn, and Bernice started to panic, but Leona and Ambrose kept calm. They seemed to like the sense of adventure, which seemed bizarre to the others. The two "braver" ones picked the most likely place where the hole in the ceiling was, and the five followed that pathway. They came around the last bend and saw another dead end. At that moment, everyone started to doubt that they would ever get out. Ambrose, finally discouraged, leaned against the wall in front of them, his back turned to it.

"Careful, bro," Dilyn said, "that wall looks a little—"

It was too late. The wall began to fall over as Ambrose unintentionally pushed it. It went toppling to the ground and him with it.

"—weak," Dilyn finished.

The group scattered to the nearest wall and stayed there, hoping to evade any coming traps. As the dust settled, they thought Ambrose was done for. They started peering in the new room when he gasped, "Guys!"

What they saw immediately caught their interest. The room they gazed in was a large, square one. It had nothing on its walls, floor, or ceiling except an excess of vines. At its center, though, was a high, rectangular, stone pendulum with a faint green glimmer emitting from its top, accompanied by a small, narrow set of stone stairs at its front. The group moved closer, looking rapidly for any traps around them. There were none.

Bernice still stayed at the doorway, just in case another wall slid into the place of the other, trapping the other four, but her friends rather bitterly assured her there was nothing to worry about.

They slowly walked up the steps, two at a time led by Ambrose and Leona. They were in unaware awe of what lay on top of the pendulum. Built into it was a basin where two glowing objects sat. They were Daggers, about ten inches long. They had black sheaths and handles with golden fittings, straps, guards, and pommels. The green glow came from inside the sheaths.

"How long have these things been here?" Ambrose wondered aloud.

"Ages, generations, centuries, maybe even millennia!" Amory said.

"I don't think so," said Dilyn. "Look, there's no dust on them. If they had been here for millennia, they'd be covered in dust, unless dust can't get on them."

"Do you think they've been discovered recently?" Bernice asked.

"Probably not," Leona answered. "If so, they certainly wouldn't be left here by whoever found them."

"Not unless they're dangerous . . ." said Ambrose, reaching out to touch one.

"No!" said Dilyn. "Don't do it! It might kill you or something!"

"Or it could all be some sort of hologram or mirage," Ambrose said. "Even if I do get killed, someone has to take the risk and see."

He slowly reached out to touch one, completely devoid of fear—or sense. He made contact. Nothing happened. He picked it up. Still nothing. The other four were packed tighter with fear than the surrounding walls were with stuffy air. Finally, he took it out of its sheath. As the Dagger became unsheathed, it glowed brighter and brighter until it was completely exposed. It then exploded into another level of bright, luminous green around them.

Amory, Dilyn, Bernice, and Leona looked back at Ambrose. No external harm had come to him.

"How do you feel?" asked Amory, making sure no internal harm was done.

"I . . . feel . . . amazing." The words slowly came out, but Ambrose was fine. "Told you."

He started to play around with the Dagger, wielding it, slashing from side to side, acting as if he was a fantastical wizard. He did, in fact, have a new, immortal power, as he discovered when he pointed it at the wall on his right. Suddenly, a green ray of light shot from the Dagger. It went to the wall and stopped before hitting it, where the ray branched out like a cone and made a bright white circular portal with a green outline. When the portal was complete, the Dagger ceased to emit the ray, and Ambrose put his trembling arm down.

They stared at it a long while before Ambrose broke out a smile at last and said, "Let's do it!"

Naturally, all four responses, oral or not, were hesitant. There were many what-ifs.

"What if it goes to a strange new world?"

"What if it goes to an even more dangerous world than this one?"

"What if it doesn't even go to another world, but it just goes somewhere else on Earth and—oh no! It's past five o' clock! Our group's gonna call the police at this point!"

"What if it doesn't go anywhere, and we'll be killed just by entering it?"

Ambrose answered them all in one sentence. "I don't know where it leads, but I know it leads out of this cavern."

"What if it doesn't?" Bernice persisted.

"Of course it does, otherwise why would these Daggers even be here? Look, we all want to get out, right? Well, this is our only way. We just have to take risks sometimes." At this, he looked at Leona. "Who's with me?"

Reluctantly, one by one, Dilyn, Leona, Amory, and Bernice agreed. Bernice grabbed the other Dagger, just in case, and put it in her left pocket. Then, together, they went in.

EPILOGUE

Azarias stepped into the Center from *Chârâsh* and knelt before the Vine, curiosity and concern in his expression. "You beckoned, my King?"

"Yes, thank you for coming, Azarias. The time has come; the war has deepened."

The cherub took a deep breath. "The multiversal war? The War of *Rôb Têbêl*?"

"Yes," Nazir answered solemnly. "Now that he's lost his hold on Liberdane, Marah has busied himself with persuading several other nations throughout the realms to follow him, even nations on which he has a loose grip."

"Of course, he persuades them to follow something other than himself, something that is appealing and right to them, correct?"

"Yes. He will use just causes and groups of 'noble' advocacy to distract the nations from me. Maewing and the Self-Worthy are on the top of his list of assets. I've called to Maewing numerous times, but she will not heed my voice. Nor will Lisias, though he passes me every time he goes between worlds. Their newfound resolve to 'save' worlds through conquest will only bring more violence. There will be many more battles both in the fields and the shadows, and that is why I've called you here. I'll be adopting several new Envoys, so you'll be quite busy preparing their equipment during that time."

"I take pleasure in nothing else but serving you in this way, my liege! Are your current Envoys ready for the battles?"

"Some are; many aren't yet. But either they will be, or they'll fall away. Don't worry. If I've already won this war, then I can certainly see to its end!"

Azarias chuckled, "How long before the Envoys are ready and the battles begin?"

"Soon."

"Ah, so any century now!" the cherub laughed again.

Nazir laughed too. "Yes, but a little sooner than that."

"Robe . . . Taybay?" Bernice sounded the name out. *A very weird name for a very weird place,* she thought.

"Yes, Bernice," Nazir said. "Weird as it sounds, *Rôb Tëbêl* is a collection of worlds. Your universe, including Earth, is just one of these worlds. There are dozens of them. I am the Creator and King of all these realms, and I know everything that happens in each one of them, because I am in them all, as well as here."

"If you're in each of these worlds, which I assume includes ours, how come no one's ever seen or heard of you?" Leona asked.

"In this central sphere, you can see, hear, feel, smell, and taste me, Leona," said Nazir. "Inside every world, though, three of those senses cannot find me: sight, smell, and taste. However, inhabitants of these realms can still hear and feel me, and many do. See how some of my branches stretch out into the portals to all the worlds? This is how I am everywhere."

"Wait," Dilyn said, "we're not the first ones here? You're saying there are other people on Earth who have encountered you? Why haven't we encountered *them?*"

"You have, Dilyn. It's just that many of them are not very bold or outgoing about it." This, the Vine said with a despondent sigh, but his voice's pace intensified. "But this time of idleness is about to end. A new day is dawning, and I am going to bring it forth—through you."

"What?" asked Amory, representing all of the group who were all a bit in shock. "Us? How and why are you going to do it through us, and what do you even mean by a 'new day'?"

"To answer that, Amory, I must explain something. Ever since I created *Rôb Tëbêl*, I have called all individuals, that they would get to know me and I them—even though I know all about them anyway—and that I would redeem them and make them complete. And afterward, that they would let me do my redeeming work throughout the realms. Many decline and even deny my calling, but some accept. These I have appointed to be my Envoys throughout *Rôb Tëbêl*."

All five kids knew that an envoy was a type of ambassador or representative. They still had questions but let Nazir continue.

"These Envoys are representatives of me in each world, and I through them fight battles, win wars, ensue peace, bring about justice and truth, and, most importantly, show my love."

"Love?" Ambrose asked, a hint of disgust in his tone.

"Yes. Love is who I am, and it is what I do. Every action I make through the Envoys is solely based on love. However, my love is very different from the kinds of love you are familiar with. My love sees the good and the bad, does not overlook either, and is powerful enough to move me to keep the good and destroy the bad."

"You said that you want to redeem people," said Bernice. "Redeem us from what?"

"Ultimately, your pride," said the Vine. "The dominating species in all these realms—which in your realm would be humans—have one common, underlying weakness: arrogance. You instinctively adopt the lie that you're better than I am. Study yourselves for a minute, and see if this is true, but you've lived your lives thus far for mainly one purpose: yourselves. You have at times been selfish, have been afraid of what could happen to yourselves, and have stolen, lied, lusted, and spent deadly words for the benefit and pleasure of only yourselves. Am I wrong in stating this?"

The kids looked inside themselves for a moment. Amory remembered all his doubts when *that* happened and recalled pondering what wrong things he had done that might have been the cause of that horrible experience. He also remembered all the times when he stole in order to get food on his table. Ambrose remembered (with a little difficulty) the companions and the two girlfriends he had abandoned and how lazy he was before developing a good work ethic. Dilyn remembered everything he had done alongside his brother and the people he had hurt. Leona remembered disrespecting her mom a time or two and recalled the lie she had told just earlier that day. Bernice remembered her selfish motives in many of her choices. She considered her passivity when she decided not to do what she should have in many circumstances. All five students lowered their heads, bearing every bit of their guilt. They were right where the Vine wanted them.

Leona decided to ask the question Nazir was waiting for since before he created *Rôb Têbêl.* "Why do you want *us* to fight battles and all that? Who and what are a few high school and college students, who are evidently evil, to you?"

They couldn't see it, because this Plant did not have a face, but they could somehow tell that Nazir was smiling. "You mean as much as everyone else in each of these worlds. You mean everything to me, so much so that I gave up everything I had, struggled with everything you mortals experience, and fought death and evil and won against it, just so I could have you." He let that sink in and watched the confidence in each of the five rise. "I have chosen you five specifically because you have talents and gifts I want to use to show my love. I created you. I know everything about you. I have gifted you, and most importantly, I love you. I gave everything to have you, and you are mine."

If any other stranger had said that it would've creeped the students out. But this Vine was different. He seemed like the perfect father, the father whom some students present wished they had. Now, Nazir asked a question he had been waiting to ask since before he made the worlds.

"Do you accept and believe that this is true? Do you openly accept my authority over your lives, and do you believe that I love you and bought you and am King over everything?"

Of course, they all hesitated. Was this real? Was it a dream? If it was, was it the kind of dream one has when he's asleep, or the kind one ponders and wishes would happen? Or was it real? They all went back and forth one time or another. Finally two people stepped forward. They were the two who never knew any true father, and they were yearning for one. They had been longing in agony for years, and now, they believed that this father could quench all of their emptiness. These two were Amory and Leona.

"I accept and believe," Leona said with tears.

"I accept and believe," said Amory, not withholding his own tears.

The very joyous Vine laughed. It was the kind of laugh a dad makes upon first seeing his newborn child. "Come here, son and daughter."

Leona and Amory walked shakily over to Nazir. Then, he did something no one had ever seen a plant do. He took his nearest two leafed branches and moved them closer to the two "newborns," and he hugged them.

It was at that point that Amory and Leona knew that they had finally found their true father. Needless to say, they hugged back. As they embraced, the young adults felt all the weight of their guilt disappear, and they felt new. They felt complete. They felt whole, and in fact, they were. It was a very eerie feeling.

They soon discovered why this feeling was so strange when they heard the other three almost panic. "Uh, what's that red vapor coming out of them?"

"It was their blood," said the Vine, whose receivers of his embrace had not budged but were still very alive. "If you noticed, the leaves I'm hugging them with have spiky edges that are penetrating their blood vessels. I'm basically ridding them of their own mortal, immoral blood and replacing it with my own moral, immortal blood."

"Oh," said the three, quite shaken over what they had just seen. But Amory and Leona seemed to want this. In fact, they thanked him for giving them his blood. Their original blood had vaporized and disappeared, never to be seen again. They were clean, and they were Nazir's children, and nothing could change that.

After the tenderness of the moment was long savored, Nazir and the children let go. Then, he turned and faced the other three who had watched the whole thing in silence and stillness. Bernice was crying with happiness for Amory but didn't see the need to go herself. Dilyn almost cried but fought back the tears lest his brother see him. Ambrose showed no emotion, as he thought a real man shouldn't.

Nazir repeated his question. "Do you accept and believe?"

They shuffled a bit, then Ambrose finally spoke up. "I can see why Leona might need you, and I don't exactly know why Amory needs you, but I don't think *we* need you."

Nazir stood still. "Bernice?"

Bernice shuffled some more, then brought herself to say, "I just don't see a reason. Besides, I don't really want to be pricked and drained of my blood today."

"Why not?" asked the Vine. "You know you'll get my blood instead, which is much healthier."

Taken aback a bit by the question, Bernice finally said, "It looks too painful. Does it hurt? It does? It's relieving, though? Well, even if there's a slight chance of it hurting, I don't want it. And again, I don't see a need to, pain aside."

"All right. Dilyn?" asked Nazir.

Dilyn looked at his brother, then said, "I'm with them," indicating Bernice and Ambrose.

"I'm right in front of you," said the Vine, almost with a surprised tone. "You have all seen my love firsthand, and you still don't believe me?"

"What's a lot of emotion going to prove?" Ambrose asked.

"Absolutely nothing," said Nazir, "but these two have finally found something that has fulfilled their deepest sorrow. My love is not founded on emotion. It is founded on action and being." Nazir paused as if waiting for someone to reply, but no one did. Then, he turned back to Leona and Amory. "Now, my children, you have been named Envoys of the Vine. Receive your equipment."

At this, two brand new branches came out from inside the Vine's thick stem. Out of the branches came large leaves, which were folded and enclosed. They reached out toward the two children, and once they were directly in front of them, the leaves opened. What they found inside was almost disappointing.

In both leaves were several particularly shaped pieces of metal. Their shapes were varied per leaf, and they looked rather odd. Along with the metal was a rolled up and sealed parchment in each leaf.

"What are these?" Leona asked.

"Metal and instructions for your weapons and armor," Nazir announced, excitement in his voice. "You will need these to withstand and end the threats within these worlds."

"So there are things in these worlds that are dangerous?" asked Bernice.

"Eh, how dangerous can they be?" Ambrose said with hubris. "Only as dangerous as a big, special plant. Come on. If these two wimps want protection, that's fine, but the three of us want to go exploring these cool new worlds." He looked at his two companions. "Right?"

Bernice looked at Amory, then shrugged, "Sure. Why not?"

Dilyn looked at everyone, including Nazir. "I'll go with my brother."

At that, they turned to go. Ambrose picked the portal that was just to the right of the one leading to Earth.

"Dilyn," Nazir said.

Dilyn turned and looked back.

"Don't let your brother's decisions determine your own."

Dilyn didn't respond. He simply turned back and followed Ambrose.

Amory grabbed his molds—as did Leona—and called out, "Bernice, wait. If Nazir says these places are dangerous, at least wait for our stuff to be forged so we can protect you."

"You don't even know how or if that's going to happen," Bernice snapped back. "That Plant might just leave you with a few bits of metal and expect you to do it yourself." She looked at Nazir, then back at her friend and grinned. "I'll be fine, Amory. What's the worst that could happen?" At that, she walked into the whiteness after Ambrose and Dilyn.

There was little silence that followed the three's departure as Nazir said, "Come, children. There is no time to waste. Your friends are walking into a fearsome danger, and they need you, but not without your gifts. There is a portal in front of you, past me, leading to a special forge where all the Envoys' equipment is made. The smith there will mold your equipment in enough time for you to rescue your friends. Now, go!"

The pair made haste to the portal directly behind the Vine (he seemed to be facing every direction). Leona practically leapt through, but Amory stopped and turned back to the Plant.

"What is it, son?"

"I just wanted to say . . . uh, I just wanted to thank you." Amory smiled, and he knew Nazir was smiling too.

"You're welcome, Amory," said his new father.

At that, Amory, engulfed in a strange peace, ran through the portal.

4

MULTIPLE MYSTERIES

B ernice, Dilyn, and Ambrose came out of the white and observed their surroundings. Overall, this world was similar to Earth. The sky was blue, containing white, puffy clouds and a bright, golden sun. Far below them was an endless field of long, green, wavy grass.

Below them! How high were they? Bernice looked at what they were standing on. Apparently it was a massive bush. They were on a giant, jade-colored leaf, which was connected to a branch on the bush. The branch, along with all the others, was gray and had an average diameter of a few feet. The three were amazed when they put the pieces together.

"Is it just me seeing this," asked Ambrose, "or are we super small?"

"Or maybe we're super big," Dilyn said. "You never know around here anymore."

"I think the world's super big, and we're the same size as we were before," said Bernice. "Those portals back there can move us throughout worlds, but I don't think they can change our size."

Then they remembered the portal! They all looked back to see if it was still there and were a bit alarmed when they found no trace of it.

"Oh, well," said Ambrose. "If there isn't any danger here, we should be fine. Come on. Let's go into the bush and see what we can find."

"But what if there really is danger around here?" Bernice asked. "What if that big Plant was actually telling the truth? What if—"

"All right, I've had quite enough of your what-ifs," Ambrose snapped. "The last time you guys hoarded me with those, I told you that these portals are safe and would lead us out of that cavern, and I was right, wasn't I?"

Bernice said nothing.

Ambrose wasn't satisfied. He wanted an answer. "Wasn't I?!"

"Yes, you were right!" she said. Her patience wasn't at its best that day.

"OK, if I was right then, shouldn't you believe me now?"

"All right, whatever. But you can't be right all the time, Ambrose."

"Why not?" he said with a smirk, then he turned to go into the bush. "Relax, Bernice. What could possibly be in here that could hurt us?"

"The distance from here to the ground," Dilyn said.

"Shut up," said his older brother.

With that, the pioneers trekked from the leaf along the branch and into the giant bush. Of course, it was a tad darker inside than it was out in the sun, but the three could still see fairly well. There were thousands of branches and thousands more leaves, all waiting to be explored by these newcomers.

"Which way, Bernice?" Ambrose asked when they came across some other branches.

"Uh, how about that way," answered Bernice, pointing to the larger stem to the right with more branches coming out of it.

So that way they went. Whenever they came to a fork in their path, Ambrose would ask Bernice which way she wanted to go, and they would follow that path. This went on a while until Ambrose just silently picked a way and the other two followed.

After what seemed like hours, Bernice began to wonder where they were actually going.

In response to her asking this question aloud, Ambrose said, "Why do we have to go anywhere specifically? Can't we just explore around without having an actual place to go?"

Bernice pondered this question and began to consider this philosophy to be faulty. The things that followed would confirm her suspicion.

They continued along Ambrose's random path through the bush, along branches, across leaves, over gaps. On a whim, Ambrose signaled to an odd branch below the left of the branch on which they were currently. What made this limb unique was that its first part was bulbous; it looked swollen. It was the same color as all the others, but there was a significant bump right next to the twig they were on and was about forty feet long. It was followed by a smaller bump of half that size.

Not surprisingly, Ambrose wanted to go on that branch, and without argument, Bernice and Dilyn joined him. As they hopped on, they took notice of the bulbs' quick and slight quiver but took little consideration. The three made their way along the largest lump.

About halfway across, Bernice began to journey to the side of it, while the Brandts walked toward the smaller swell. She stopped before she could slide off its rounded edge, and she realized that there were four small branches coming from the two lumps. She made her way to the other side. Another four. She then looked at the small swell, on top of which were the two brothers. They were gazing at something embedded in it.

"Hey," said Dilyn, "check out these shiny black rocks in this branch!"

It was then that Bernice realized it. She gasped, but it was too late. The thing they were on began to move, both lumps and its eight "branches." It violently shook its back end, launching Bernice into a nearby branch overhead. It then thrust its head up, throwing the two brothers into the air and then down onto the real branch in front of the large creature. They then realized that those weren't rocks; they were eyes.

When Bernice caught her breath again, she screamed what was now obvious, "It's a spider!"

———

When Amory and Leona got through the white, they found themselves exactly where Nazir said they would: a forge. They could identify a few items around them: an anvil with several hammers and other tools, a large furnace for heating, a cast if necessary, and a couple of barrels of oil for cooling and hardening. All their surroundings looked very gray, and it was all lit by a few meticulously placed, simple chandeliers. They also noticed there were several weapons and sets of armor on display and many racks to display them. Except for these and the forgery equipment, this place seemed very empty.

After they wandered around a bit, Leona thought to say, "Did Nazir say there'd be a smith here?"

"He did," said Amory, "but I don't see anyone else but you."

Leona then decided to call out, "Hello?" It was loud enough to cause echoes to bounce around to and from the equipment.

Apparently her voice was heard. There was a clanging, and slowly, one figure emerged from around the right corner. Amory and Leona stepped back in fright, for the creature before them was unlike anything they had ever seen.

He was huge, about seven feet tall. He had a very noble and strong face that was mostly shaven except for his black sideburns. His long head was draped in black hair stretching below his shoulder blades. From those shoulder blades came two large and aerodynamic silver wings. Another pair of wings, looking stronger than the other pair, emerged just beneath. These two robust wings were armored in a dark silver, shield-like metal. They covered his body and formed his armor. It was not like medieval armor; rather, it was smooth and flexible—as would be any wing. His arms, the only other parts of him exposed, displayed muscles Amory could only hope to have.

The creature welcomed his visitors. "Greetings, children." His voice was very deep, and even its sound seemed enough to crush a man. "What, or who, brings you here?"

After a bit of stuttering, Amory said, "Nazir the Vine brought us here." He then showed his metal molds, and Leona followed suit. "He gave us these and brought us here to get them molded."

"Ah," uttered the still, heart-stopping voice, the mouth out of which it came forming a smile. "So Nazir has deemed you Envoys. Of the multiverse, is it? Then let's not waste any more time." The giant creature paused. "Welcome to *Chârâsh*, the forge of the Envoys of the Vine. I am Azarias, the keeper and forger of this realm. Hand me your metal and instructions, and I will have them ready for battle in no time."

The duo hesitated. This creature was very intimidating, and he wanted their armor and weapons. Could they trust him? Was he *really* going to make their weapons, or was he going to steal them and do something terrible to them both? They then thought of Nazir, how he gave them fulfillment and peace, and his promise that there would be a smith there to get the molding done. Since they saw no one else around, the two trusted Nazir and the creature and gave him their pieces.

"Excellent," said the massive being. "Let's make your weapons!" With that, Azarias set off to the furnace. He said this furnace had a special heat source: the throat of a phoenix. The students from Earth hesitated to believe this, but their skepticism was vanquished when the oven suddenly came to life with extreme, white flames. He requested their names, and they each gave them, both first and last names. Azarias took Leona's metal first and put them all in the furnace's mouth, then unsealed the instructions and examined the sketch on it. The pieces quickly began to melt, and he took them to his rather large anvil, grabbed a hammer, and started beating and bending them into shape. Every strike changed the scorching metal drastically. He then turned down the oven's heat and placed the products back in.

Leona had more questions. "Uh, how long have you been here?"

"Oh, a little less than a millennium. Nazir appoints a new weaponsmith every thousand years."

"How long has it been since you've made a weapon?"

"About an hour."

"Really?"

"Yes," the creature said, "I like to make equipment as often as I can, so as not to get out of practice. Nazir saves and fulfills people every day. When I'm not making their equipment, I'm making something for practice and for pleasure."

"Nazir said there are others who have encountered him, but they aren't outgoing," Amory stated. "Are they Envoys?"

"Yes, because they are still his children, and all of his children are meant to represent him wherever he sends them. Some *are* outgoing, but they have been called to stay in their world. He calls a select number of individuals to be Envoys throughout the multiverse, which means he works through them in multiple worlds. This is your calling, and—" He looked in the furnace, carefully pulled out some of the pieces with a pair of pliers, and submerged them in the oil barrel. Large flames arose and travelled up the heat-treated metal pieces. Azarias pulled Leona's pieces out. "—You have accepted the calling. But the calling of an Envoy in the multiverse is no more significant than that of someone meant to stay in their own world."

As he quenched the rest of the pieces in the oil, Leona had another question. "How do people from our world get to Nazir? We got here using two mystical Daggers, and I don't think other people come the same way we did."

"They don't," said the creature. "Usually, people from your universe, and those from the other universes, either are led by other Envoys to Nazir or they sometimes come through small cracks or cervices in landforms, which bring them to Nazir. Nazir himself makes these entrances, and does this to everyone and calls everyone to accept him and then forevermore grow in him. Some accept, many don't. Some even accept and then forsake the Vine and the calling later."

"So he makes alterations in nature to bring people to him?" Amory asked.

"Around here, who's to say what's an alteration and what's not?" said Azarias with a grin. "As I understand it, those Daggers came from a couple of Envoys many centuries ago who decided that battles and continuous growth and discomfort was not what they signed up for, so they buried the Daggers in a cavern near Philadelphia. I know this because Nazir told me. Those Envoys might have forsaken him, but he has a plan for everything. He usually gives a Dagger to every Envoy so they can access him, but I suppose he provided them differently this time."

Azarias dried the pieces off, sharpened the weapons with a tough stone wheel, and finished the armor. All of this happened in a matter of minutes.

"The work is complete," he said, then courteously gave the work to its owner.

Leona looked at her gifts. She put them down to observe them individually. She got a gold helmet, which was small yet comfortable, and a purple breastplate with shin and arm guards and lined with silver. On the left of the collar on her breastplate was a small badge with a crackly sort of icon.

Azarias briefly went into a closet and returned with some brown boots and a belt to go with them. Her weapon was a small axe, whose handle was purple and whose head was like silver, all lined with gold. The two axe heads on either side were very thin and short, and their origins on the handle were two adjacent origins instead of simply one. It looked like a crooked, single-handed pickaxe.

"It seems a little small," she commented, a tone of complaint in her voice.

"As I forged it, it looked like the mining axe of a dwarf—" Azarias began.

"Ouch," Leona said.

"—But you are much taller than any dwarf I've met. If your height were any different, the weapon would not be right for you. This axe is yours alone, Leona."

She said nothing and began to put her armor over her purple hoodie and gray pants. As she did this, Azarias turned to Amory. "Now, let's get *your* equipment ready!"

With that, the creature inserted Amory's pieces in the furnace and opened Amory's instructions. As he watched the massive smith work, Amory began to really admire him. Like Leona, he too had questions.

"So there are dwarves in these worlds too?"

"Yes. There are many creatures throughout the realms. Some you have only heard of, and others you have never heard of," said Azarias.

"What is the emblem that Leona has?"

Azarias grinned and said, "It is the emblem of the Envoys. It is the image of a root, resembling us being rooted in the true Vine, Nazir."

"What is the name of the metal Nazir gave us?"

"It is a very unique metal," said the creature. "Its components will not be found in any of the worlds. It comes from Nazir only. It is called *Charisma*. It is easily bent into the proper shape, but once it is quenched," he said this as he doused Amory's equipment in the oil barrel and took it back out, smoke and fire arising from the product, "it can never be broken or bent."

"*Charisma* . . ." uttered Amory. "Interesting name for a metal. It kind of sounds like the name of this place, Ka-rosh."

"Yes, *Chârâsh*. The names' similarity is no accident."

Soon, the smith completed his second task in a very similar timeframe and proudly declared, "The work is complete."

Amory examined his equipment. He also had a small helmet, a breastplate, and guards for his limbs, as well as boots and a belt—except his armor was blue, lined with gray, and his leather (at least, what he thought could be leather) was gray. He received an Envoys' badge as well. His weapon was a large, gleaming sword. Its blade, being double-edged, was long, sturdy, and straight. The hilt was blue and gray, and from the golden pommel branched two symmetrical D-guards, whose tips touched the handguard between the blade and the hilt.

It also came with a deep blue translucent sheath with straps connected to it by buttons, like the buttons on a jacket. The sheath was about four inches wide at the beginning three inches but then swelled after that and measured about six inches wide, making it seem to have a handle of its own. The sheath was also lined with another layer of silver metal along the outside.

"Lucky you," said Leona, "You get a big sword and I get a puny little axe."

"Do not underestimate the power of Nazir through your gifts," said the now grave creature, "nor should you compare your gifts with another's." He then turned to Amory. "Judging by this sword, you are meant to be the leader of a certain group of the Envoys in the multiverse."

"Leader?" asked Amory. "I thought Nazir was the leader of the Envoys."

"He is," was the reply, "but he has called you to be a leader between him and the Envoys, a channel of authority from the King to his representatives, and therefore, to all his people. All Envoys are called to be leaders and trailblazers, but every so often, Nazir calls certain people to be an example to them of what a leader should be. Such a calling he has placed on you, Amory."

Amory was not only hesitant but resistant. "How do you even know this?"

"Because with your sword comes a legend partially fulfilled, as with your weapon, Leona," began the smith, "legends which I cannot tell you until you rescue your friends."

"What?" Leona said suddenly. "We have to wait—and survive—to hear these legends? Why?"

"I was commanded to reveal the prophecy to no less than the five of you. Now, hurry and save your friends, bring them to Nazir, then get them back here. Only then will the legend be told."

With that, the two now fully equipped Envoys turned around toward the entrance of the forge, *Chârâsh*. They then realized that the portal entrance had vanished.

"Where'd the portal go?!" Amory said in a panic.

"Don't you have those green Daggers?" asked Azarias.

"Oh, no," said a now pale Leona. "They have them both."

5

THE FIRST ADVENTURE'S COMPLETION

Amory almost cursed under his breath. "I completely forgot! Now I really regret letting Bernice go through; she had the other Dagger!"

"Can't you help us get back to Nazir?" Leona asked desperately, looking to Azarias.

"I thought you'd never ask!" the creature said, and he took an odd-looking, twenty-five-inch-long Sword from a propped sheath hidden behind a rack of other weapons. The hilt was wooden, with a straight, silver, double-edged blade coming out. Out of the hilt's sides came two green, curved, supposed decorations. They looked like thin D-guards, except they stretched from the bottom of the hilt to the middle of the blade. "This Sword has the portal-summoning power taken from the Daggers of the Cosmos. The Daggers were made specifically for transportation between worlds—from one Cosmos to another. Their power rules this weapon. It has the power to merge worlds and make them all one. But in the wrong hands, it would lead to multiversal ruin."

Azarias pointed the Sword at the same place where the kids' portal had left them. Suddenly a glowing green ray of light—very similar to the ray emitted by Ambrose's Dagger yet much brighter—shot forth from the blade. It came to a stop and branched out to make a new portal in place of the old. When the ray stopped emitting, Azarias put the Sword back in the place he found it.

"Why is that Sword hidden?" Leona asked. "Is someone after it?"

"Perhaps another time, I can tell you," was the reply. "Go and get your friends! I'll see you soon."

Leona and Amory hurried through the portal, looking back once to see the creature smiling kindly, then all they saw was white. They finally saw some form of the center and sprinted to it.

"Hurry, guys!" said Nazir as they bolted past, "and bring them home!"

It was an odd thing to say, but Amory and Leona knew exactly what he meant. They remembered which portal their friends had gone through and entered it. As they waited for the white to wane, they couldn't help but feel anxious of what to expect.

Bernice kept screaming warnings to the Brandts on the branch below, trying to keep them aware of the giant spider's multiple, devastating blows from its sharp legs, as well as its savage attempts to simply scoop one or both of them in its mouth. The large gray monster combatted Bernice's warnings with its own horrible screeches, assaulting Ambrose and Dilyn with every movement they made. Any dodge they made only put them in danger of another split-second attempt by another leg to puncture them. Somehow, they were able to continue dodging without getting killed in an instant, though they didn't know how long they would be able to keep up.

"Ow!" Finally, a hit. Dilyn, in trying in evade another leg, got cut by the leg coming down on him. Now, his left leg was beginning to bleed and swell.

Ambrose, trying to make his way to him, received a scar in his right arm, and the same result occurred. *Its legs must have a poison,* he thought.

From then on, the two brothers repeatedly got hit by the great spider's legs, and the inflammation from their scars worsened. The swelling wasn't as puffy as it was painful, and the brothers' movements were gradually slowing.

Bernice's warnings remained in the air until she remembered: the Daggers! She felt for the one she took in her right pocket. At first she felt nothing, and she began to panic even more. Then she felt some more. It came to her memory that it was in her left pocket. She felt around, desperately hoping that it hadn't fallen out when she had been launched onto the branch she was on now.

At last she snatched it and then tried to think of a way to summon a portal where she and the Brandts could all escape without the spider following them through. She finally decided to put the portal remotely in front of the spider, where the brothers could (maybe) easily get to it, and where she could climb down to it. She pointed the glowing Dagger in that direction, and its glow increased.

Abruptly, she was smacked by one of the spider's dart-like legs, and she flew into another more distant branch. She began to feel a stinging in the arm holding the Dagger. The Dagger! Where was it? Bernice looked frantically around for it, until she finally spotted it on a leaf far below her, even below the branch on which the Brandts and the spider were. She started to climb her way down toward it, quickly enough so she could get it soon, yet stealthily enough so the great arachnid wouldn't catch her again.

Ambrose saw that Dilyn was trying to fend off two or three legs at once. The elder brother escaped the leg he had currently been fighting and ran to help his younger brother. Underneath the spider's massive body, he approached Dilyn from behind.

Evading the legs, Ambrose pushed him away so that Dilyn was behind the spider and closer to the branch they were on before they had jumped onto the beast. The branch was high enough for him to run underneath and also low enough so the spider could not fit through.

"Run!" Ambrose said, and Dilyn began to bolt for the safety point.

The spider turned around and saw Dilyn and started to chase him, tripping up Ambrose in the process, sending him off the twig on which they were fighting. Fortunately, Ambrose had grabbed onto the ledge, his body dangling in midair. Thanks to his fitness, he could hang for a while, but he saw that his brother had endangered himself again.

Dilyn ran under the overhanging branch and watched fearfully as the spider walked around it, giving low-pitched shrieks, trying to find a way to catch its prey. Observing as the fiend came closer and closer to him, Dilyn began to panic.

"It's not gonna get you in there!" said Ambrose, still hanging.

It was too late. Dilyn already decided to rush out the other side of the hideaway and make a run for another branch down below.

"No!" Dilyn heard his brother cry, and he looked behind him to see the gray spider had crawled over the overhanging branch and was now rapidly pursuing him.

Dilyn ran as swiftly as his panicked legs could take him, but two tiny legs against eight massive ones would never prevail. The terrible beast snatched him in its jaws and tried to swallow him in its rather small, toothless mouth. Dilyn kicked, punched, scratched, squirmed, and screamed with all his might but could not get himself free.

At that moment, he heard two yells. They were human, and they sounded as if they came from valiant warriors. In an unexpected way, he was right, for he saw Leona and Amory leap down from a higher branch and assault the massive creature.

Amory landed on the head and started slaying away with his new sword, and Leona landed right in front of Dilyn, who was still half-engulfed in the fiend's mouth. Amory pierced one of the spider's eyes, and it let out a deafening shriek, which was Leona's chance to take Dilyn by the hand and get him out of his snare. Then, she had an idea.

"Stab another one!" she said.

Another shriek, and she ran up to the beast's mouth and began to slash it from the inside with her axe, which was indeed just the right size. With one final blow, she used her axe as a hook to lead the spider's head, along with its whole body, off the edge of the branch, releasing her weapon as the monster began to fall. Amory jumped off the spider's back just in time and landed safely beside Leona and Dilyn as they watched the beast plummet down the bush, breaking several branches on the way down before finally hitting the ground, dead.

"You all right?" Leona asked Dilyn, visually examining his swollen wounds.

His first thought was *yes*. He was indeed still alive, though he checked to make sure. His actual response, however, after seeing the scars himself, was, "Maybe. I don't know."

"A little help!" they heard, and the three of them ran to where Ambrose remained hanging. Amory offered his hand, and with some effort, Ambrose let go with one hand and took it.

"Never thought you'd need me, huh?" Amory said. He only got a glare in return. "Where's Bernice?" he continued.

Ambrose looked back at him, a sudden look of concern in his expression. Amory imitated his expression and began to search for her and call out.

"Bernice! Bernice?"

They had barely searched for a minute when they heard a swift spark of noise. They turned to see a green ray of light coming up from a branch below them, forming a new portal. The four ran to the right edge of their branch—the two brothers with a little difficulty—to see the origin point of the ray, after the portal was created and the ray retreated. They found Bernice standing on a leaf a few feet underneath them.

"Are you OK?" Amory asked.

"Yeah," she said. "Is there a quick way up there without going around multiple branches?"

The group of four turned and looked around for a long, yet relatively thin twig onto which she could grab. After a bit of seeking, Dilyn found one suitable enough. Amory took it and reached it out to Bernice. She too grabbed hold, and he with Leona pulled her up (the Brandts were now too weakened to pull much of anything, though Ambrose never admitted it).

"That armor turned out nicely," Bernice said.

"Thanks," Leona said. "Now it's time to get yours!"

"Ours?" asked Ambrose. "We still don't need any! We're fine! We were doing fine without you."

Amory was about to argue, but he didn't have to. Bernice did instead.

"And if they hadn't shown up, you wouldn't have a brother anymore. Look at yourself. Look at Dilyn. Look at me! Without them, who knows where we'd end up!"

"One little scar, and you're complaining and fussing again," said Ambrose. "I've got a couple dozen, and I'm fine! I'm not complaining! I can take it. I don't need any help! I don't need you!"

"When are you going to learn that you alone are not enough?" asked Leona. "What's it going to take?"

"A heck of a lot," he said, though he did not actually say "heck."

It was after he said this that they entered the portal and disappeared from that death-filled place. After their argument, no one held a decent mood, but when Nazir appeared in the white, they became more solemn. Leona and Amory grew enough joy to form smiles on their faces at the Vine's presence, but the other three became more fearful than their last visit. They waited for him to scold them and say that he told them that there was danger, but they were instead surprised when he exclaimed, "Welcome back!"

There was a short silence, then he beckoned the three. Bernice, Dilyn, and Ambrose stepped closer, while the other two stepped away. Leona and Amory didn't leave, but they gave them all some space.

"How was your exploration?" asked the Vine.

As low as their heads were before he asked that question, they dropped even lower following it.

After a moment, Bernice said, "It, uh, went fine for a while. We landed on a really big bush and walked around its branches. Then, we walked on this really big thing, which turned out to be—"

"Just a really swollen branch," said Ambrose.

Bernice gave him an appalled glance, but he returned another that basically communicated that if she told Nazir the truth, she would later regret it.

"It was very interesting," said Ambrose. "I've never seen anything like it. You've got some pretty cool worlds around here. I'll give you credit for that. Anyway, we were about to explore your world some more, but these two," pointing to Amory and Leona, "insisted that we come back."

Bernice, Dilyn, and the others waited to see what Nazir would do. He did nothing for a moment. Then he said, "Your arms and legs look a little larger than the last time we met. You've grown that much already?" He, of course, was being sarcastic, for he knew all about their misadventure. He was testing them.

Ambrose couldn't find a good lie quickly enough, which gave Bernice the opportunity to speak up. "The big swollen thing was a giant spider, sir." Ambrose gave her a very mean look, but she gave him none in return. "It attacked us, and that's how we got swollen. The spider's legs had venom on the tips. I'm sorry we didn't listen to you!"

Bernice began to cry, and Nazir serenely hushed her. Dilyn, who had remained silent this whole time, again fought back tears of his own. His big brother made no move or sound at all, though when Dilyn looked, he did seem a tad flushed.

After things went silent again, the Vine said, "Would you like me to heal your scars?"

"You can do that?" asked Ambrose, his head lifting in unison with the others. They all said yes.

Nazir beckoned them forward more, and with a touch on each of them with one of his sizable leaves, the swells started to decrease until it was as if they were never there.

"Thank you," said all three.

Nazir brought back his leaves, and they backed up to where they were before. Then came the same question he had asked before: "Do you believe in me?"

Again, there was a hesitation and a silence. The affirmation in answer to the question was something for which Nazir so longed, as did Amory and Leona now. They were so anxious for their friends to say yes, to receive the gift, the redemption of their wrongdoings and salvation from their just doom, the freedom from pain caused by both themselves and others. Finally, a reply.

"Yes," uttered a voice which, much to the delight of Amory in particular, came from Bernice. "I accept and believe."

"Out of fear," said the Vine, "because of the awareness of danger, and that you think I'll protect you from it? Or because you want redemption from your mistake of not taking me seriously? Or for redemption from your mistake of fear?"

After a moment of thought, she said with tears, "Yes. All of the above. I'm sorry for not trusting you. I do realize that I will be hurt a lot more without you than with you. I believe in you, and I believe you can and will redeem me."

"Come here, daughter," said an overjoyed Nazir.

Bernice came a breath's distance from him, and he hugged her in the same way he had earlier done with Leona and Amory, even replacing her blood with his—inwardly cleansing her of all her mistakes and regrets and quenching her every need. Through tears and one long breath, she hugged back, showing her trust and gratitude.

Afterward, Bernice went to join her two fellow Envoys, who eagerly embraced her.

"Welcome to your new start!" exclaimed Amory behind his own tears.

They watched as Nazir turned to face the Brandts. "Anyone else?"

Ambrose shuffled back and shook his head. "No thanks."

"Still nothing?" the Vine asked. "You still think you can make it on your own, even though I told you that you cannot take credit for your own life?" There was a great sigh. "I won't give up on you, Ambrose. I have special plans for you, just like I do with everyone else present."

While there was no response from Ambrose, Dilyn looked at him, looked back at the Vine, then back again. "Can I?" he asked Ambrose.

"Sure, whatever," said Ambrose. "I don't care. If you think you need him, go ahead. But I don't need him."

Interiorly grieved at that lie-influenced statement, Nazir said, "That's not his choice, Dilyn. It's all yours. Do *you* accept and believe in me?"

The young freshman nodded. "Yes. I accept and believe."

Nazir was convinced, but he wanted to make sure Dilyn was. "You believe that I can take away your faults and regrets forever? That I can make you new, and I can make you like me, but also fully you and not anyone else?"

"Yes," was the answer.

Nazir laughed joyfully again. "Come on over, son."

Dilyn came over to the giant Vine, and Nazir did to him what he had done to Bernice, Leona, Amory, and to countless others in the millennia past. He redeemed him. He remade him. Dilyn had never felt freer in all his fourteen-year-long life.

As soon as it was finished, he called Bernice back over. Then, he stretched two leaved branches toward them. He opened the folded, green leaves and revealed Bernice and Dilyn's metals and instructions. They smiled at the sight of this, knowing that they would somehow become like what their two companions were wearing and holding at that moment.

They saw that their set included two more of the fantastical Daggers. "The two you have now belong to Leona and Amory," said Nazir.

Bernice gave the one in her hand to Amory and took her own. Ambrose hesitated to give up the one he had.

"Why?" he asked. "What if I don't want to? I would if there were other ways to explore these worlds."

"There are," said the Vine, "but that Dagger doesn't belong to you."

Ambrose took the Dagger by the blade and slapped the handle into Leona's hand. "I'll just find another way then. I'll let you know right now that I have no intention of becoming one of your puppets. Sorry, but no."

Ambrose expected to see some external sign that he'd hurt the old Vine's feelings. He didn't.

Dilyn, for once ignoring his brother, examined and took his pieces. They looked quite like how the previous ones had. Bernice's appeared comparable as well, except her set included a large, soft, golden, durable-looking cloth. Etched in it was the symbol of a root.

"What's this?" she asked.

"It's a flag with the Envoys' emblem," said Nazir. "I have chosen you to be the Envoys' flagbearer."

"But I still get an actual weapon, right?"

"Follow Amory and Leona into the Envoys' forge, and you will see." Then, the Vine grinned. "I can't wait for you to discover the gifts I've given you! Go on!"

At his excited bidding, all five of them went into the portal to the forge, led by Amory and Leona. Ambrose looked back at Nazir to see if he would keep him from going in, but Nazir said nothing, so Ambrose went in after the rest.

———

As Dilyn walked into the alleged forge, he observed his surroundings. There were racks of eerie weapons and armor everywhere. The gray brick walls made it all look a tad spooky, but not all too frightening, even though those overhead and wall-connected fire lamps were the only sources of light.

Dilyn also saw a lot of forging equipment in front of him and his friends. Some of them he could identify, such as the forge and the anvil . . . *Wait. Who's that at the anvil? In fact, what's at the anvil?!*

"Welcome, Envoys!" greeted the towering creature.

"Hi, Azarias!" said Leona. "Good to see you again!" Then, she turned to the three unarmored individuals whose eyes were wide with fear. "This is the Envoys' smith, Azarias. He'll make your weapons and armor. Azarias, meet Bernice Banner, and Ambrose and Dilyn Brandt."

"I've heard much about you three," said the being in his booming voice. "Welcome to *Chârâsh*, the forge of the Envoys. Are you ready to see what gifts Nazir has given you?"

"Yes!" said both Dilyn and Bernice after overcoming their hesitations.

Azarias stretched out his hands to receive their molds, and they excitedly placed them into his care. He then turned to Ambrose.

"Where is your metal?" he asked.

"Didn't get any," said Ambrose, curious to see how the creature would respond.

"Must not have accepted Nazir yet, then," Azarias said. "Oh well. There's time, and if there's one thing I know about Nazir, it's that he has a plan for everyone."

Ambrose narrowed his eyes and tilted his head slightly as the smith turned to the new recruits.

"Now, to make your armor and weapons! We'll start with Bernice."

Azarias took her metals and put them in the large, phoenix-fueled furnace. He startled the newcomers as he lit it and it exploded into life. He laughed, as did Leona and Amory this time. After viewing the instructions and giving the metal time to heat up, he took the pieces out one at a time and pounded them on the anvil with his intimidating hammer. As Azarias worked the metal, he struck a conversation with Bernice.

"So, you were chosen to be the flagbearer."

"Yeah, I guess so. What specifically does that mean?"

"It means that you are meant to visually represent and lift up Nazir's name wherever you go, be it a battlefield or in a time of peaceful celebration."

"Huh," was the utterance in reply. "That sounds boring and hard."

"The life of an Envoy is never simple, or at least shouldn't be," Azarias said as fire flickered from the first oil-quenched piece. "But it is always worth it. And it's only boring if you make it so."

Before she knew it, Azarias had finished her pieces and ended in saying, "The work is complete."

Bernice gazed at her awesome orange armor lined with silver. The helmet, breastplate, limb guards, and brown boots and belt were satisfying to her eye. What she was not entirely proud of was her weapon. It was a shining, silver spear with an orange rim, around which Azarias had attached the golden flag.

"Is this my weapon?" she asked.

"Indeed. Nazir wants to ensue victory through you, Bernice."

"With a flag on a stick," she said.

"As I told these two earlier," said the creature, "never underestimate the power and potential of the gifts Nazir has given you. He has given you what he knows you can be dependable with, and he can bring about impossible and indescribable things regardless of the unequal quantities of your gifts. What matters is the quality, and the quality of all your weapons comes from him."

He let that sink in a bit, then turned to Dilyn. "Your time's come. Are you ready?"

"S-sure," he said.

At that, the mysterious being wasted no more time. He took the metals and placed them in the still-blazing oven. There was more hammering, more quenching, more sharpening.

During this time, Ambrose began to admire some of the apparatus he saw displayed on the racks around him. He then had an idea. He subtly snatched a saber that was fancy in appearance. He glanced over the gleaming, double-edged, twenty-five-inch sword with the wooden handle and long, green D-guards/blades. He thought it looked like a portal-making blade. He found a sheath of a softer material that looked like a good fit. He carefully slid the weapon inside, then put the sheath inside his left pant leg and tried to hide the blade as best he could.

An honors student and valedictorian, but I can't hide a freakin' sword, he thought.

Finally, Azarias said, "The work is complete," and Dilyn looked over his new gear.

He had green and gray armor, and each part looked and felt a bit comfortable. His weapon was more impressive than he expected. It was a bow. It had a stained wooden handle in the middle, out from which two curved spokes came. Attached to both tips was a durable string. Azarias had gone behind a corner and returned with a green quiver almost overflowing with arrows, complete with a strap to go around his torso.

"Is this for me?" asked Dilyn.

"All yours," was the answer he heard. "No one else's."

"Thank you," he said.

"Wow," Leona said, "you guys get the cool weapons and the big roles, while I get a little pickaxe, and Bernice gets a simple spear."

"This has nothing to do with gender," said Azarias, "nor are any of your gifts simple. They each possess their own unique abilities, and it's your choice—and Nazir's—to use them to whatever extent. I told you before, and I'll tell you again: your gifts are more complex and powerful than you think. Just when you think your equipment from Nazir has reached its limit, and you think there's nothing new or fresh about it, you will discover something new about it that you had never before imagined."

"That reminds me, you had something to tell us after we got back, Azarias," said Amory.

"Ah, yes. The legend of which I told you. Well, before I tell you about this specific prophecy, I must explain that Nazir is everywhere, which he likely already told you."

"He did," said Dilyn.

"Well, not only is he everywhere, but he's also everywhen."
The five looked confused.

"He is everywhere in time; he is in the past, he is in the current, and he is in the future."

The students began to understand.

"With that in mind, Nazir has predestined the purposes of all his Envoys, along with all beings. He has planned out every step of their paths. He has ordained and written out the destiny of every single one of his children. For every Envoy, there is a legend, and he knows how each of your legends end because he's already there!"

The Envoys and Ambrose got comfortable and listened intently.

"You each have an individual legend which belongs only to you, and all of your legends coincide with each other because Nazir created you to work, serve, fight, and love together, alongside each other and for each other. You were made to be a team. Now, I cannot tell you everything about this legend, because I myself do not know, but what Nazir told me I will tell you."

The kids leaned closer. They could not stand the suspense much longer.

"The underlying and collective legend, as I know it to be, is this: When Nazir chooses a score of diverse beings, and those beings choose him in return, he will, ultimately through this twenty, bring about an awakening like *Rôb Tëbêl* has never before undergone. This will be the sign to confirm these individuals: the main leader will possess a great, blue sword, one will have a great bow, one will wield a thin, double-sided axe, one will bear the Envoys' flag with a spear, one will bear a giant hammer, one will have the ability to destroy weapons. This is all I know so far, but it goes further."

They all sat silent for a moment, taking it all in. They wanted to believe that they were something special, as Nazir had said, but they weren't sure they were ready in any aspect to do what Nazir wanted. Finally, someone noticed a flaw—at least as he viewed it—in the prophecy.

"Wait, by 'a score,' you mean about twenty people?" Ambrose asked. "I only see four Envoys. Unless of course you mean *I'm* included, in which case, I'll have to remind you that I am not a so-called 'Envoy,' nor do I intend on becoming one anytime soon. Were you implying, though, that *you're* one of them?"

"No, I am not one of the prophesied individuals, nor are any of my kind," said Azarias. "My species is sometimes called the cherubim; I am what you might call an angel. As you might have noticed, I am also not an Envoy. I started out as a servant of Nazir, and I have never forsaken Him. I am constantly with him and know him very well. Therefore, I am continually amazed by those who actually see him less than I do yet have more faith and loyalty toward him than I could ever have."

"Ah," said Dilyn. "So do you know what our individual legends are?"

"No, I don't," the angel said. "But Nazir does, and in his timing, he will allow you to discover your full potential, and he will carry it through."

"We can't even fulfill our own potential?" asked Leona.

"No. Your destinies are far too great for any mortal to bring forth! Only Nazir can do that, and rest assured that he will. What I can tell you about all Envoys' destinies is that ultimately, he will make you perfect, flawless. You will become like him, seamlessly reflecting his image. You are called to do so now as his representatives, but until the end, you will still have faults. When that day comes, though, you will be perfect and made worthy to live with the King forever because of his redeeming blood in your veins."

After another moment of contemplation, Amory changed the subject. "I still don't get why I'm supposed to be the leader."

"Neither do I," said Azarias. "I don't know anything about you, except that you love your friends, and you carry the sword foretold by Nazir himself. Only he knows why he chose you, and he has plausible reasons."

"Of course, I love my friends! They're all I've got!" Amory glanced at his new friends, who did not know what he was hiding. He then looked at Bernice, who had known this secret for years. "I can only lead myself. I don't know how to lead anyone else!"

"You should take this to Nazir. He knows better than I. You should know that if you are ever struggling with anything, be it any kind of internal battle, or even a physical one, you can call on him, and he will be there with you and listen to what you have to say, and he will be victorious over your battle in his timing. It would also be wise to afterward listen to what he has to say."

There was an even longer, almost agonizing quiet that followed. Finally, after several minutes, Azarias said, "It's almost time for you to go. Before that, I must tell you something I have told all the Envoys who have come here. You, as Envoys, are like your weapons. You will be put under extreme heat, banged and smashed on every side, ground, hardened, and sharpened ultimately by none other than the Vine himself, who prunes his branches. He will bend you into the shape he wants and take off whatever is unnecessary until he makes you a finished product, a tool for his use, ready for his perfect work."

"Are you talking metaphorically?" asked Dilyn. "Because I don't know if I want to be ground and beaten."

"As far as I know, yes, this image is metaphorical. But again, I don't know exactly what Nazir has in store for you, except for one thing for right now, which I now send you to him to discover. Farewell, and I'll see you another time, be it the Vine's will."

"See you later, Azarias," they all said in their own, quiet ways.

The five walked through the portal which Bernice made, one at a time, each in a sense of awe, silence, and contemplation at their legend. As Ambrose began to fade, Azarias noticed that the boy's left pant leg was very stiff and wide, but even though he wanted to, the angel neither did nor said anything.

When they got back to the center of the multiverse, Nazir again greeted them. "Welcome back! Wow, do you four look sharp! Your equipment looks great on you."

They said their thank yous, and afterward, Amory said, "Azarias said you have something for us to do."

"Yes, I do," said the Vine. "It is a special mission that all Envoys must accomplish."

"Where are you sending us to battle?" asked an excited Leona.

"No, not a battle. Not yet, though that day will come soon. Right now, I want you to go back home and get back to your normal habitats. Back to your families, to your friends, your schools, and your country."

While they were disappointed that they couldn't get on a battlefield yet, they were kind of relieved that they supposedly were to go back to their comfort zones.

"So, all of this was pointless, almost like a dream?" asked Ambrose.

"No," the Vine said. "You're going back to your own environments, but I want you to live differently than you did before. I have redeemed you. I want you to live like it. You have been reborn, and I want you to grow and mature a little more in me before I send you to other worlds. It is my hope that you do come and see me frequently, as that is key to your growth. You're not supposed to go back to comfort. You'll never grow that way." He turned slightly toward Amory. "If you have anything with which you're struggling, I want you to come to me so I can fix it. I don't want to just help you with it, I want to repair it altogether. Do all of you understand?"

"Yes," they all said.

"All right, now off you go."

As they went, quietly and a tad despondently, Nazir further said, "I'm extremely glad you came. I'll see you all soon!"

They walked through the white, anticipating what might've happened in their own world while they had been gone, or if any time had passed at all. Amory went first, then Bernice, then Dilyn, then Leona, then Ambrose.

Just before Ambrose went through, Nazir said sarcastically, "You're limping in your left leg, Ambrose. Did I miss a spot when I healed you?"

There was no reply.

PART II

THE WILDERNESS

6

THE SELF-WORTHY

A mbrose and Dilyn stumbled inside to the kitchen to get a
cup of water. The Brandts' kitchen had gorgeous granite
countertops, and guests had always thought their vanities were
made of real silver. The two brothers didn't really take notice of
this. They had just come in from a tennis match on the court
in their backyard and were exhausted.

After getting a drink, Dilyn silently went to his room.
Ambrose figured he'd be going to see Nazir again. This had
become quite regular. It seemed that ever since their adventure
two weeks ago, Dilyn had been visiting that weird Plant every
day, though Ambrose had noticed that he skipped a day or two.
For a split second, he thought of joining his younger brother,
but he just as quickly dismissed the idea. He didn't need healing
today.

Ambrose sat in his favorite armchair and took out his
phone, glancing through social media, looking for anything
new or remotely interesting from his friends. Maybe one of his
friends had posted a new selfie. Nope. Nothing new. Nothing
special. He saw a picture of Bernice, with whom he had become
"friends" on social media. Then he scrolled down further, though
his mind was no longer there. He began thinking back to their
return to Earth.

The five friends had thought they would end up in that mysterious underground cavern in Amory's property, but they didn't. They found themselves in the forest, right next to the hole where they had entered the cavern. They somberly and quietly made their way back to Amory's house and rode back to the Eagle Hotel, where the three from Craghill said goodbye to Amory and Bernice. When Ambrose, Dilyn, and Leona finally reunited with their school group, they received very harsh words from their leaders. The severest of all was, "What in the world are you wearing?" referring to Leona and Dilyn's armor and weapons.

Leona, taking the question literally, said, "Lifesaving equipment."

"Well, I don't know where you got it, but you don't need it now," said another leader. "You can take it off now."

Dilyn had rather hurriedly taken off his, but Leona stubbornly kept hers on. This enraged the leaders enough to shout, "Take it off now, or you will need it!"

She slowly and awkwardly obeyed, then returned to her room. According to orders, she was not to be heavily involved with the kids for the remainder of the trip, especially with Dilyn and Ambrose. The leaders thought she had too much of an influence on the two boys. All three of them quietly laughed at that.

Leona did not easily obey others who are wrong, even if they do have authority over her, Ambrose recalled in his mind.

Ambrose's mind returned to the five-hundred-square-foot living room. He thought again of Dilyn going out of this world to talk to Nazir. Maybe Nazir thought he was ready enough to go on a mission now, and Ambrose was missing it all! This made Ambrose more frustrated. Then, he remembered what he had brought from his adventure in the multiverse: the Sword.

How could I have not used it yet? he thought. *Well, things have happened one after the other since we got back. The rest of the field trip, the arrangement for the engineering job at the trade school, the apartment I'll move into soon....*

Ambrose got up, walked quietly to his room, and shut the door. He passed his queen-size bed, sports gear, and computer desk and opened his closet. The closet was a room all on its own, and there was enough space for him to walk in more than ten paces. He found the pile of laundry containing sports jerseys and formal khakis. He moved the pile somewhere else to reveal the Sword it had been concealing. It had been over two weeks since the return home, but the Sword did not look any duller than when he had first seen it.

Ambrose picked up the twenty-inch blade and admired it. The blade seemed to shine a bright white and the D-guards a luminous green. This was odd, Ambrose thought, because his closet had no windows.

He then got an idea. Pointing it in front of him, he wondered if it would summon a portal like an Envoy's Dagger would. Ambrose watched as the guards got brighter and greener, as did the blade. A blinding emerald light shone off the Sword until a ray suddenly burst from it, almost launching Ambrose back. As he had assumed, a portal was being formed.

He stood still for a moment after it was complete, and the ray retreated to the Sword but only for a moment. Ambrose looked around, back out to his room, making sure no one was watching, then took a deep breath. He strode through the portal, through the white, and found himself surrounded in black.

What? Where is Nazir? he thought. He then saw a few sources of light shaped as short semicircles. He realized that those were bottoms of the portals to the other worlds and that he was in the multiverse's center after all. The partial gateways lit up certain areas in this underground place. In it, Ambrose saw nebula-like plant roots in the dark soil, which looked so much like outer space. He also saw that, in the bowl-like bottom of the spherical center, there were passageways throughout the ground where he would have to rummage to find specific portals to get to certain worlds.

Ambrose simply chose the entry in front of him. He knew it would be a new world, and he was beginning to get excited. He even thought he was going around Nazir, doing something without the Vine noticing! This, of course, was not true. Unbeknownst to Ambrose, Nazir even knew what happened underneath him because his presence remained (he could sense things with his roots). Ambrose climbed to the portal and squeezed through until he could stand in the white.

After coming out of the white, Ambrose found himself in a very strange place. It was similar to Earth, with a cloudy sky above him, solid ground underneath him, and plant life everywhere. The strange thing was that the greenery was not green at all—it was blue . . . as blue as your yard when it's been sprayed with poison. Ambrose saw blue grass, blue leaves, and blue shrubs. He was dumbfounded at this "bluery."

Ambrose looked slightly ahead of himself and saw a glowing stream of yellow. As he got closer, he saw that it was a perfectly square line going in a certain direction but frequently turning. It looked like a bright road stripe on Earth. He stepped on it several times and heard a deep boom with each step.

Must be a path indicator of some kind, he thought.

Ambrose scanned the far distances around him. He was in a long plain, which stretched in front of and behind him. To his right was a thick, blue forest, and to his left, he beheld a most astonishing sight. It was a towering, high-tech city with odd-shaped structures, some measuring easily one or two hundred stories. Some buildings looked like jewels, others appeared as uncut crystals, and others still looked like ingots. The tallest building was a complex one, consisting of several thin, twisty, intertwining towers. Each tower's individual levels looked like a vertebra, so each tower was a different orientation of a spine. Some of them did not look like human spines.

With the shape of those towers, I'll bet that's a big financial district or something, thought Ambrose, and he went to get a closer look.

As he approached the city (which lacked outer walls of any kind), he caught glances of some of the people inside. Many of them were not people at all. There were some humans, but he also saw elves, dwarves, gnomes, giants, fauns, minotaurs, centaurs, and creatures which he could have never even imagined. In addition, he thought he saw one or two cherubim, though they looked much creepier than Azarias—yet they were charming at the same time.

One five-foot-tall faun with silver armor exited the city and caught sight of Ambrose. As the swift, intimidating creature approached, the new visitor could not help but feel like running away at a moment's notice. Other than Nazir and Azarias, the only nonhuman being he had met before was that giant spider, and he didn't know how hostile all the other beings were. As the faun got closer, though, a smile broke loose on its face.

"Hello there!" he greeted enthusiastically. "Welcome to the city of Laves, in the world of Ourrance. My name is Lisias. What is yours?"

"Uh, Ambrose," he said, a tad more comfortable.

"What brings you here?" asked Lisias, glancing at Ambrose's Sword with a half grin.

"Uh, I had taken this from, uh, *Chârâsh*, I think . . . yeah, the place where Azarias, that angel, works. Oh, you probably haven't heard of him."

"Oh, I have indeed heard of him," the faun said with a slightly smaller grin. "He is quite the noble warrior. You mean he didn't see you take it? He doesn't exactly let people take his weapons freely."

"Evidently not," said Ambrose. "Anyway, I took it to my world, that's Earth, and just kept it in my closet for a couple of weeks. I just now got it out and used it to get here."

"Incredible," murmured Lisias.

"What's so incredible about that? It's not much of a story."

"Ah, it matters not now. But do you know how special that weapon is?"

"Not really," Ambrose said, "I only grabbed one I thought was fancy."

Lisias turned and began pacing a little. He seemed to be thinking deeply about what Ambrose said, all the while quietly repeating the word *incredible*. This went on for a few awkward moments until he finally turned around with a homely smile.

"You know, I have a friend who knows the exact value of this Sword," he said. "She can tell you just how wealthy you are in possessing such a treasure."

Of course, Ambrose liked the sound of that. He readily agreed, and Lisias began taking him west of the city, on a path going straight from the entrance Lisias had just used. They followed one of the bright yellow lines, which the faun said was a stream of light energy illuminating the path. After being asked, Lisias also said that the plants were blue because the chlorophyll makeup here was different than on Earth. What makes plants green on Earth is different than that in Ourrance, and it makes the vegetation in Ourrance blue.

They went on into the forest that Ambrose had earlier seen and strode on for several miles. They finally arrived at their destination, and Ambrose's mouth gaped open at the sight of it. It was a gorgeous, towering castle with whitish-gray stone bricks making up the walls. It was decorated with intricate, black banners and paint designs. It had twelve turrets throughout, each going six stories high. As they approached the front drawbridge, Ambrose noted that it was wide open.

"Y'all aren't very protective in Ourrance, are you?"

"No," the faun said. "Here, you are welcome just about everywhere, but especially in this fortress. The queen of this castle is always gracious and open-armed."

"Is she the queen of this whole world?"

"Heavens, no!" the faun chuckled. "Whoever heard of anyone ruling an entire world? No, she is the queen of her cause. She does not call herself a ruler of any kind, but we, her followers and friends, do."

"What is this cause of hers?" asked Ambrose.

"Come inside. She tells it best."

They entered the fortress and found thousands of beings of all worlds and races—unarmored at the moment—filling a very wide hall. This room, which seemed to take up the whole first level of the castle, looked old-fashioned with its décor, but with its lights, yellow triangles in the ceiling, it appeared bright and lively. Lisias took Ambrose through the crowds to the middle of the great room where a small centaur, which appeared to have wings, was talking with a few of her friends: another centaur, a dwarf, a human, and a cherub.

"Maewing, your highness, we have a visitor."

The white-winged centaur, who was only under seven feet tall (which is short for any horse or centaur), turned to meet the newcomer. A look of giddiness, yet authority rose on her face.

"Dear Lisias, please stop calling me 'your highness.' I'm a person, the same as you."

Ambrose gazed at Maewing with wonder. The hair on her head and her horse body was deep black, and she was wearing white chain mail, horse armor, and a silver breastplate. She looked young and energetic, yet also considerably wise. She interacted with everyone around her as if she was equal to them. Lisias was right; she did not act like a typical queen.

"And who might you be?" asked Maewing with a very friendly tone and smile. "And what have you got there?"

"My name is Ambrose," he said rather calmly. The fact that she didn't act with much authority had eased him. "This is an interworld teleporting Sword that I took from *Chârâsh*. Lisias here told me you could tell me its value."

"Oh, indeed I can," the small centaur said. She extended her open hand toward the weapon. "May I?"

"Oh, yeah. Sure," Ambrose said. As Maewing examined it, he asked her a question or two. "No crowns or thrones?"

"No. I always say that we are all equal. I don't call anyone here my servants, troops, or representatives. If I call you anything of mine, I'll call you my friends."

"What specific kind of creature are you? I mean, I've never seen a centaur with wings."

Lisias answered this question with admiration. "She is a winged ponytaur. Her kind was extremely rare in her day. The winged ponytaurs were the elite warriors of her realm. Sadly, she is the only one left. She might look young, but she is 534 years old. That is a large amount of accumulated wisdom."

"Wow," said Ambrose. "Your kind doesn't age much, does it?"

"You could say that." Maewing smiled. She gave the Sword back to Ambrose. "That Sword you hold is one of immeasurable value. I don't know if you know this or not, but this Sword has the power to bring worlds together. It can enable anyone to have unlimited access to each world. It has the power to unify the multiverse!"

Ambrose was speechless. He gazed again at that marvelous treasure in his own hand, which looked even more marvelous now that he knew what it was. He was also humbled. Should a random person such as himself have such power? He wanted to ask what to do with it, where to keep it, how to properly use it. Maewing answered before he even asked.

"I suggest you hang onto that. Perhaps hide it somewhere safe—safe enough that no one even knows about it. Just save the Sword until you need it. And don't worry, I can tell you when to properly use it if you bring it every time you come here. Now, to change the subject, I suspect Lisias told you about my cause."

"He only said you had one. He didn't say what it was."

"Well, ever since I was young—and I mean even younger than I look—I had always loved the aspect of self. We are each unique, and there is something that we can each contribute to these worlds that no one else can. We must learn to see ourselves as such, and then strive, even fight, to make that contribution. We must prove to the multiverse who we are and why we are needed.

"I have been fighting for this cause for centuries. My goal is to convert the entire multiverse to individualism. I want the worlds to know how special each individual is, and I want to see each society functioning as if every single person is valued and included. Everyone you see in this castle—and many more in other worlds right now—is part of my group of friends. They have been shown how special they are, and they are willing to fight for themselves, for their rights, and for their honor. We call

"Yes, but she had to return with the original," said Sevi. "It is mandatory that all doppelgängers remain with their twins for life."

The march finally restarted, and Ambrose, with Ives at his side, proudly led the procession. If only his Envoy friends could see him now!

ourselves the Self-Worthy, because we know we have the ability and the right to live for ourselves. No one else has deemed us able but ourselves. We have deemed ourselves worthy."

Ambrose stood there with proud, gleaming eyes, yet with a bit of hesitation. He had always hoped that he could make a difference in his own world. That's why he worked so hard in school and saw those great results. He hoped that being at the top of school would put him at the top of the workplace. Then, he would be able to use his influence to promote good. But here, in this other world, his goal seemed so much closer.

"Why would you need to fight?" he asked. "This idea sounds pretty acceptable to me."

"You'd be surprised by how many worlds see blended, blurry groups as better than each person's contributions and talents. They are the harder ones to convince, even to the point of violence."

Ambrose paused for a moment or two. He had to process it all, though it seemed he had known this all along. He liked the idea of him being so valuable to society, and he loved the idea of proving his worth to others, including that Plant, Nazir. But wait. Hadn't Nazir told him and the others that they were worth everything to him? The memory was blurry now. If he had, then that would just prove Maewing's point. To Ambrose, it all boiled down to this: he could change the world, and he could prove wrong anyone who thought differently. He didn't think Nazir thought differently, so maybe this idea was true. But who said Nazir was right? In fact, who said Maewing was right? For now, it might be best to assume both are right until it could be proven otherwise. Ambrose simply did not know enough to oppose Maewing now.

"Umm . . . how do I become one of your 'friends'?" Ambrose finally asked her.

"You already are," she said in a delighted tone. "Welcome to the Self-Worthy, Ambrose!"

A large group of creatures came to the new self-appointed recruit to welcome and congratulate him. Ambrose, though confused, politely and even excitedly thanked them all, especially Lisias. Then, he turned back to his new leader.

"OK, what now? What do I need to do as a new member?"

"Stay here with us," said the ponytaur. "Develop friendships with us, so our unity will be strong. It's always nice to fight and advocate alongside comrades, you know."

"Wait," said Ambrose, "I have a family—parents and a brother—at home. They'll probably be wondering where I am. Actually, I'll be moving out of the house in a couple of weeks. Could I do that, then come here? Then there'll be less concern of where I'm at."

"All right," Maewing said. "I think it'd be best to do that. Good thinking, human."

———

Ambrose set off with his Sword to return to Earth and settle the arrangements. Boy, could he not wait to come back! Maybe before then, he could talk to Dilyn and bring him to meet this legendary leader. Yeah, that would show Nazir! A transfer from one group to another! From that point on, Ambrose set all his thoughts and efforts in returning to Ourrance. He wished he could go back sooner, but more than that, he wished to tell his friends the Envoys about what he'd found.

— 7 —
VISITING NAZIR

T he smell of an omelet could be sensed for miles. Amory poked his head out of an open window in the kitchen, looking around at the dense, lush forest scenery. He had a lot on his mind. He had been regularly visiting Nazir for over three months since he had become an Envoy. Today, after breakfast and before school, he would go again.

As he looked at the green displayed in front of him, he remembered returning to that cavern that had held the Daggers a few weeks ago. He had stood there, at the hole where he and his friends had entered, wondering whether or not he should go back in and see what else was there. It was dark inside again, as the fire in the oil basins had gone out. Amory had decided not to go in, assuring himself that all that was there now were deadly traps.

Amory presently went back to making his breakfast then cleaned the kitchen (he always did this before eating). The omelet, filled with ham and multicolored peppers, along with cheddar on top, satisfied whatever hunger he had. The earl grey tea lifted his spirits too. With a final swipe of his napkin and gulping a quick glass of water, he headed for his bedroom.

Before going to the Center, Amory put on his armor and strapped on his sheathed sword. From his antique nightstand, he took his well-used and polished Dagger. It glowed even better than when he had first seen it, probably because it was being used frequently again. Usually, before he summoned a portal, Amory would do a little twirl with the Dagger, adding a hint of spice to his sometimes-redundant routine. He didn't this time. He might have even texted Bernice so they could meet up in the Center with Nazir. Not today. Amory wanted to be alone with him. Something had weighed on his heart and mind for months, but up until now he had never gotten the courage to bring it up to the Vine. He was determined to do it today.

He walked slowly through the portal and the white, as he had done countless times before. Amory saw the large, ominous Plant getting closer as he approached it. Finally he was in the center of the multiverse again.

"Hey, Amory!" came from the delighted voice of Nazir.

"Hi," the young man said timidly.

Nazir sensed immediately that his child was not acting normally. "What's on your mind, son?"

For quite a long time there was silence. Amory was set on saying it, but something held him back. Perhaps he didn't want to upset the Vine. Maybe he was just afraid. He didn't know what it was, but for a few moments, nothing could come out of his mouth. Nazir stood there, silent and still, and Amory could tell he was listening intently.

"W . . . well, I just wanted to . . . well, I don't. . . ." He couldn't figure out how to say it best or how to say it at all. Finally he sighed. "Why me?"

"Why you what?" Nazir asked patiently.

"Why did you pick me for a leader, Nazir? I mean, I don't know anything about leading. I've been living on my own for years. I can only take care of myself! Everyone I've ever known has either taken care of me too or abandoned me!"

At this point, he stopped short. He thought he would start crying, and he eventually did. The twenty-two-year-old man finally dropped to his knees and wept before the King of the multiverse—and he let him. Those memories and emotions had not shown themselves in a long, long time, and when they did at that moment, they exploded. After a few minutes, Amory settled down a little, as Nazir placed a large leaf on his shoulder.

"What your parents did to you was wrong, Amory."

Amory looked up when he said this because he had never been told this before, at least not that he knew of. Now he was listening intently.

"But I can use the worst of circumstances to create the strongest and most beautiful individuals. What you taught yourself in those years of loneliness, I want you to teach to those I put under your care. Responsibility, perseverance, work ethic, strength, courage. These things are what you know well, but those whom you'll lead currently do not. I don't want to tell you everything; some of it you'll figure out. But know this: I have a purpose for you being a leader."

Amory digested it all, and it took another few moments before he asked something else: "What specifically do you mean by *leader*? We've talked about it, but what exactly *is* it?"

"When I say leader, I mean someone is meant to serve the group of which he's in charge. All leaders must put everyone else before himself and also must put me first of all. Azarias told you this before, but you are to be a channel of my authority. I lead you, and you lead others; my reign passes through you to everyone else.

"A leader is responsible for the actions of not only himself but those of his team. If one of your people makes a mistake, you take the blame. When your whole team experiences triumph, you receive the least glory. You are the least in the group, and you take the brunt of the discomfort and hardship. In addition, a leader must be strong and bold and have a spine. He must be confident in his King, his own beliefs, and then his actions. He takes the initiative, makes a decision, then acts on it, considering the best interests of his King and his team. Now, you may not have all these traits yet, but you will in time. I don't just see you as you are now but as all you will be. I see you in your full potential.

"It is also important to remember that all leaders—be they kings, senators, dictators, employers, or parents—are appointed by me. It is critical to respect and submit to them, with the solitary exception that they order you to do something that goes against me. Do you understand all this?"

"Yes, I think I do," said Amory. "Um, what if the others don't accept the fact that I'm the leader? What if they don't like how I . . . we . . . do things?"

"That's a good question, and I'm glad you asked it, because that will happen. Now sometimes, it will be because you are right, and they are jealous. They might disagree with you, but if you're doing what I said, then you're doing the right thing, regardless of who likes it or not. Other times, there will be disagreement because you'll be wrong, and the others will try to correct you. If you're not doing what I say, then it's your responsibility to see that, to listen to their corrections, and to get back on track. It all comes down to whether you're obeying my orders, if you're submitting to my authority. It's your job to know the difference."

After contemplating that for a moment, Amory said, "All right. I'll do my best."

"Of that I have no doubt," said Nazir. "Now, speaking of submitting to my authority, I need to inform you that you and I have an enemy. Long ago, one elite cherub in my kingdom decided he wanted to have all the authority and glory that I have. Because of this, I banished him, but not before he had convinced a third of the cherubic armies to join him. Now he lurks in the shadows, making sure he's not seen, causing confusion and chaos. He convinces people, through individuals and through 'special groups,' that they don't need me, that something else—including themselves—is enough for fulfillment and a successful life. But you know all too well that they do need me to purge them of their pride and their proven guilt, to make them new and achieve their potential for them."

"How dangerous is this enemy, and what's his name?"

"His name is now Marah, and he is very dangerous. He possesses celestial power, but it's a distorted version of it. You haven't seen Azarias fight, but I'll tell you that he can hold his own against some of the mightiest beings. Well, Marah could beat Azarias. He can also put up a strong fight against the other archangels."

Amory had guessed at the answer already, but he had to ask: "He's not stronger than you though, right? Could you beat him?"

"Oh, yeah. And I already have, and still am. Yes, Marah is an enemy but not my rival. He doesn't stand a chance against me, and he knows it. For now, Marah is on a leash. He's allowed to do some damage to others, and he can tempt you to disobey me. However, no temptation of his is impossible for you to refuse if you look to me. Now sometimes, you will be put in situations—not temptations—that are completely out of your control, but that's so you can learn to depend on me to get you on the other side, stronger than before. All that to say, watch for Marah. If you're tempted to do wrong, to act on your own agenda, chances are he's talking to you, and you must use the weapons I gave you to fight him off. All Envoys' weapons, soaked with my power, can defeat Marah if you'll use them right."

Amory, feeling strengthened by the fact that it was possible to win against this terrible being, looked at the sword Nazir had given him and smiled.

"Now, it's about time you got back to your universe. I don't want you to be late for your classes," said Nazir. "I'm glad you came to see me again, and I'm glad you asked the questions you did. I love it when people want to learn more about me and how much I love and empower them. Do you feel stronger than you were before you asked these questions, Amory?"

"Yes, I certainly do."

"That's because you *are* stronger," the Vine said with a smile. "See you later, son."

"See you, Dad."

The University of Philadelphia gets quite busy on Fridays. Assignments are turned in, tests are taken, and everyone wants the weekend to come just a little sooner. Such was the case for

Bernice. She had five classes to attend that day, and she was preparing for tons of relaxation when it was all finished. At long last, the school part of the day was over. Bernice quickly left the arts and science facility and almost jogged down the sidewalk to the parking lot.

"Hey, Bernice, wait up," came a familiar voice from behind. Bernice knew this voice but not as well as others. She looked over her shoulder to see Edna Dinh catching up to her. Edna, the black-haired junior with all the latest urban outfits, was in some of the same classes as Bernice and Amory. They were mostly just acquaintances, but Bernice knew quite a bit about her. Edna was the only child of a couple of immigrants from Vietnam. Her dad's job took them across the country, and they moved frequently. Because of this, Edna had been homeschooled all her life. By the time she graduated high school, her family had ended up on the East Coast. Edna was different in many ways, so not many people knew much about her other than these things.

"Hi, Edna," Bernice said. "What's up?"

Edna looked even more tired than Bernice felt. "I kept forgetting to tell you this, so I was kind of getting desperate. I just wanted to let you know that you seem to be acting different lately."

"Oh?" said Bernice, not knowing whether to be offended yet. "How so?"

"Well, I feel like you've been acting . . . kinder than you had been last year. I mean, you're more considerate of others, and you're much more sociable."

"Really?"

"And it's not just you," Edna said. "I've also noticed it in that other guy, um . . . Amory. You've both changed, and I wanted to let you know that I see the difference, and I like it. I also wanted to ask what caused the change."

Bernice thought it was the sweetest thing for Edna to come and tell her this, and she took it as an encouragement that she was obeying Nazir well. Bernice deeply argued with herself on whether or not to tell Edna about how she and Amory were different.

What if it's not the right time? she thought. *Could I botch it all just by telling her too early? Yes, I could, but is this too early? After all, she did ask, and it would be wrong not to answer truthfully.*

After spending a few awkward moments of hesitation, she decided to tell her. Nazir had been teaching her about this lately, and she felt like it was for this specific purpose.

"Well," Bernice said, "there is a reason why we're different. A really special reason. Now, you might not believe this, and you're going to think I'm crazy, but this is not the only universe that exists."

"That's not so surprising nowadays," said Edna.

"Well, it's true. There are several universes out there. And in the center of them all is this very special place." Bernice paused to make sure Edna was still interested. She was. "In this place is this giant Plant . . . a talking Plant. He calls himself the Vine."

"Really?" said Edna with a more sarcastic tone.

By now, Bernice was sure she was losing her, but she continued anyway. "His name is Nazir, and he says he's the King of the multiverse, and he's proved it more than once. I believe him. He proves that we're basically evil and doomed to an eternal death, and also he proves that he can take away all the evil inside us and make us clean and new. After that, he makes us his Envoys: his special representatives to carry out his work, to tell others this same story, and to bring peace and joy to every world."

She was finished. Edna still looked interested, shockingly. Bernice thought she had ruined it somehow. The junior's eyes looked down as she processed it all.

"Would you like to meet him?"

"Yes," Edna said, "yes, I would like to see him."

Bernice smiled wide. "All right! Oh, shoot . . . I forgot my Dagger at home. I use a special Dagger to get to him, but I don't have it. Here, let's go to my apartment and we'll go from there."

"Oh, you don't have to do that," said Edna with a grin. She pulled from her pocket part of the hilt of a Dagger that looked just like Bernice's. "Come on. We'll go behind the library. No one'll see us there."

Bernice, still in a state of shock, began to follow her. "How did you get that?" she finally asked.

"I saved coupons. How do you think I got it?" Edna whispered.

"I know, I know. It's just . . . I never knew you were one of us."

The two students got behind the college's library and double-checked to make sure no one was watching. Edna made a portal and they ventured through.

———

Edna and Bernice caught sight of Nazir, their King and their friend.

"Welcome, daughters!" he said. "What brings you here today?" A simple question with an odd answer.

"Bernice and I decided to visit you together, Nazir," said Edna confidently.

"I can see that," the Vine chuckled. "What made you decide to come together?"

Boy, Bernice thought, *he sure knows how to pick people apart.* "Well, honestly, Edna had come over to tell me how differently Amory and I had been acting lately, and I decided to tell her that you are the reason, like you and I were talking about."

"Very good, Bernice," said Nazir happily. "How did you get here?"

Dang it. "I used *my* Dagger," Edna said slowly.

Before Nazir asked anything else, Bernice finally admitted, "Because I didn't have mine on me. I'm sorry. I'll try to remember to keep it with me at all times."

The Vine was silent for a moment, then said, "I also see that neither of you are wearing your armor. Why not?"

Both Envoys quickly looked at themselves, then looked slowly back at Nazir. They said nothing at first, trying to figure out the reason. It wasn't that they didn't know but that the reason was so instilled into them it was hard to dig out.

"We, uh . . . people don't usually wear armor to school and work," Edna said.

"Amory and Leona don't seem to mind," said the King.

"Yeah, and Amory gets mocked and laughed at, and I'm sure Leona does too," said Bernice.

"So?"

The armor-less Envoys had no immediate response to that remark. They had to dig a little deeper.

"People don't generally like being mocked," Bernice said. "That means we're. . . ." Then she understood. "We're being abnormal. We're not acting like everyone else."

"Exactly," the King said. "I am not like everyone else, and since you are my representatives—my branches, if you will— you should be like me, and therefore be different than everyone else. I know you both have been acting like I want you to, and I commend you for that. I now want you to take it a step further and wear your armor regularly."

"It's hard, though," said Edna.

"I know it is. But remember, I was mocked too, and I still am today. I can hear multitudes of voices taunting my name, and I want to change their hearts through those willing to represent me. Edna, I bet Bernice didn't even know you were an Envoy until she saw your Dagger."

"Yeah, that's true."

"Wearing your armor and your Daggers can help with that. I'm not saying you should flaunt the fact that you're Envoys, but that the difference in your behavior and even your appearance can point people to me. I know that you don't usually need armor for school, but it's for more than just protection from mortal beings. Marah and his soldiers constantly have their eye on you, and they want to distract you from me. He sometimes does this by giving you an illusion of something that seems like me but is not. Once that thing fails you, which I never will, you'll think I'm unfaithful, and you'll want nothing more to do with me. That is why wearing your armor is so important. It keeps you connected with the real me and disconnected from

Marah's deception. In addition, other people can question you about why you wear armor, and you can lead them to me!

"I'm telling you this because I love you more than anything else, and I want you to love me more than anything else . . . including your societal norms. If I can train you to step past the lies injected into you, then you will indeed become mighty Envoys. That's what I want for you. Actually, I can see you there already. I can literally see you in your full potential because I am indeed already there.

"Bernice, I see you as a courageous and virtuous woman who would make me known when no one else would. Edna, I see you as a strong, uplifting woman, always fighting for others before yourself."

The three of them fell silent for a long while. The two daughters slowly digested all the teaching they were fed, and the King waited until they were ready for his news.

"All right, you two. I think you all have grown enough for the next step! Bring Amory, Dilyn, and Leona back here, fully armed, and I will tell you what must be done next. And Edna, I want you to join their group. You five are the start of a team of Envoys I will use to bring about eternal peace to *Rôb Têbêl*, and I am excited, as I hope you are!"

"Oh, we are, very much so!" the two ladies said together. Finally! After months of teaching and training, they were ready for the next step: going on missions! Bernice and Edna simply could not wait to get back; although, there was always that lingering anxiety of not knowing what that next step was.

8
DOPPELGÄNGERS

B ernice, Dilyn, Leona, and Amory, along with Edna, fully
armed, equipped, and eager, had gathered in the Center
with Nazir. When they got there, they immediately wondered
who this fifth person was—who was of course Edna. She was
wearing bright yellow armor with silver lining and white boots
and straps. Her weapon was a large gold and silver hammer
with a long cylindrical head in front and a curved, catspaw-like
blade in the back. It looked like a typical work hammer, only
supersized and more elaborate. Everyone gazed admirably at it.

"Who's this gal?" asked Leona.

"I'm Edna. Nazir said I'm supposed to join your group."

"Well, good to have you with us, Edna," said Amory, who
had already known her to a small extent. "I didn't know you
were an Envoy."

"Yeah, I have been for about four months—a little longer
than you, I guess. I haven't been the best representative I could
be, but I'm working on it." At this, Edna gave the Vine a grin, as
she was sure he was smiling too.

"Well, then I guess you are the fifth person of the twenty
that the prophecy mentioned," said Leona.

"Which prophecy?" Edna asked.

"The one where Nazir will do something to awaken the multiverse, or something like that. It said he would do it through a score of people. It seems you're the fifth one! You've got the big hammer it mentioned."

Edna raised her eyebrows and stuck out her lower lip while nodding. "Sweet!"

"All right, everyone, gather closer," called Nazir in a thunderous voice. "Bernice told you all to come because I have something to tell you: you are ready to move forward!" He paused here to let the five celebrate a little. It was a big deal for them as it was him. "You have learned and trained well. You have worked very hard, and the results are showing! I'm extremely proud of all of you.

"I am now sending you all to a battle . . . with yourselves. Each of you has an otherworldly twin, called a doppelgänger. These are your evil selves, whom I killed when I defeated evil. They must be killed so that they can do no more harm to others and so you can most effectively represent me. I am good, but they are evil. One cannot represent both good and evil, so oneself must come through, while the other is put away.

"These doppelgängers have two lives, though. I killed them the first time, and now you must finish them so they will never influence you. You will find that they have a hole in their hearts where I pierced them. You have all been practicing with your weapons and Daggers as instructed, so you're ready. You must stab them in the exact same place for them to die; it must be the heart. The portal to my left leads to Ourrance, a very wealthy world, and to a city where your other selves live. Go there, and you will find your doppelgängers. Any questions before you go?"

"Yeah," said Dilyn. "Will they have weapons of their own? I mean, will we have to fight them?"

"Would you fight if you knew your last life was at risk?" asked Nazir.

"Yeah, I guess I would."

"But no, they don't have weapons," Nazir said. "They used to have some similar to the ones you have now, but I took them away when I killed them the first time."

"Does it have to be us who kills our own doppelgänger, or can we help each other?" asked Amory.

"Yes. You can help each other fight your twins, but you must kill your own evil self. That's the only way it can work."

"Do we have what it takes to beat them?" asked Leona.

"Because of the strength I alone give you, yes."

"But what happens if they defeat us instead of the other way around?" Edna asked.

"Then you become just as evil as them. You will still be Envoys, but not good, effective ones. Don't let that happen."

"How do we not let that happen?" Bernice asked.

"You must use your Daggers to pierce the wounds. Even your arrowheads, Dilyn, are too large to fit through. Use your other weapons to get close enough and subdue the doppelgängers, but use your Daggers to finish them."

There were no more questions. After a brief silence, Nazir proclaimed, "All right, off you go, my young warriors! Remember, I am always with you."

At that, they excitedly and confidently marched through the white.

As the five friends entered the strange new world, their eyes widened at the sight of it. Blue plants, yellow-lit lines, and . . . was that the city Nazir had mentioned? Its gem-shaped structures were enough to catch anyone's eye.

Few words were spoken as the five Envoys made their way toward the city. Even though Nazir had given them a large amount of information, they still had no idea what was in store and how exactly they were going to execute their mission. Leona and Amory had felt this way before when they were sent to save their friends from the giant spider, but the others had not yet had this anxious feeling.

Finally, they reached the borders of the city. Someone (they didn't see who) exclaimed, "Hello, and welcome to the City of Laves!"

The five thought it odd that there were no defensive walls or gates but that the streets and buildings and people were left exposed. And such people! The Envoys caught sight of centaurs, dwarves, elves, fauns, cherubim, and other humans, to name a few creatures. There were all sorts of forms of transportation as well. Some strolled on foot, others rode what resembled bikes, others had horse-drawn (or centaur-driven) carriages or chariots, some drove cars, and others still flew with jetpacks or speeders. The Envoys also noticed that some of the beings—many of them, actually—were walking or riding with a darker, more distorted version of themselves. The five agreed that this is what doppelgängers must look like.

After walking a good distance into the city, Bernice stopped them and asked, "All right, what's the plan?"

"I think we should split up and cover more ground," said Amory. "If anyone finds a doppelgänger that looks like one of us, uh . . . text us. Hide from them, while keeping track of them, and send everyone else your location. We'll all five team up and fight them one or two at a time, depending on how many you find."

"Where do we look?" Dilyn asked.

"Try the hotels or neighborhoods or something. Ask around and see if anyone's noticed someone like you."

Everyone agreed to this plan and started off, each on a different street. When they inquired passersby, the Envoys found that many of the people spoke different languages, some with sounds the humans wouldn't think possible to make. Everyone they asked who spoke English didn't help much anyway. The Envoys soon found themselves wandering around further and further away from each other.

———

Amory found himself in a spacious blue park. Everywhere he went, he got stares because of his armor and weapons, but he didn't mind so much anymore. He was starting to smile to himself until he came across an eye-catching man about his age.

The other man looked almost exactly like Amory except for his slouching stature, his defensive complexion, and his fearful eyes. This man was also wearing armor, except it was black, and he was unarmed. Amory also could not see a Dagger strapped across the other man's front or an Envoy's badge on his shoulder. There was, however, a dark hole in the left side of his breastplate and chest.

When the other Amory first caught sight of his double, he stopped short and even stepped back. Then, he seemed to muster up some confidence to smirk and step forward.

"I've been waiting for you," said Amory's doppelgänger. "My name's Yroma, what's yours?"

"Amory," said the original as he began to circle his rival.

———

Leona found her way to what looked like the town square. There was a multicolored stone fountain, sidewalks and roads with those golden lines, and azure grass and trees, along with many groups of extravagant flowers. Leona felt she would enjoy this place much more if she didn't have someone to look for and kill. She was approaching the fountain in the center of the area when she heard someone with a familiar voice call her name.

"Hey! You there. Haven't I seen you somewhere before?"

This voice had a taunting tone to it, the kind Leona knew well. She looked behind her to see a woman in black armor walking toward her. This woman looked unmistakably like Leona, except for the armor and the fact that she had no weapon. The other Leona confidently—and almost smugly—came closer to the original. Leona now saw the black hole in her doppelgänger's armor and upper shoulder and noted that she had no badge.

"No, I don't think we've met," said Leona hesitantly. "My name's Leona."

"Mine's Anoel. Nice to meet you."

In saying this, Anoel extended her empty hand. Leona never shook it.

———

Dilyn had managed to travel to the complete other side of the city and was now in a large crowd of pedestrians. This area seemed the wealthiest part, as it had the tallest, brightest, and strangest buildings. Dilyn tried to figure out what each was for, but soon gave up. He had a mission to accomplish, and he had to focus.

Suddenly, he bumped shoulders with a kid in the crowd going the other way. He turned to apologize but instantly became awestruck. The other kid gave a nervous, overdone apology for him. This kid was the spitting image of Dilyn. The other Dilyn kept walking the opposite direction, and the original turned around and followed as closely as he could, going against the crowd's current. He subtly texted everyone his location (somewhat amazed that this place offered an otherworldly form of Wi-Fi), trying also not to lose his target.

Dilyn and his doppelgänger finally broke free from the crowd, and Dilyn could now see him better. His double, called Nylid, was also wearing black armor. As Dilyn watched Nylid walk along, he noticed that Nylid's demeanor was very insecure and fearful, which made him all the more dangerous. It is difficult to kill someone who is afraid to die (again).

After about ten minutes of striding, the twins found themselves in a slum-like neighborhood. The houses were much less interesting, and what few people there were seemed to be silent and stone-faced. Dilyn kept following his doppelgänger, trying to think of a way to penetrate that hole in his chest.

He then saw that Nylid had a rock in his hand, but he noticed a little late. Nylid suddenly turned and hurled the jagged stone at his pursuer. Dilyn sprinted to the right just in time. He rushed for cover behind one of the homes.

"Listen, w-w-we can work something out!" he heard Nylid say. "I haven't done anything to harm you—until now at least."

Dilyn knew that was a big fat lie. He took an arrow from his quiver and crept around the house.

Edna had found her doppelgänger, Ande, in an apartment. Edna had been checking all the hotels and apartment buildings for any of those "evil twins." Her heart jumped when the landlord at this building said there was a woman who looked just like her. Edna had ridden the elevator fourteen stories up to get to her double's room. The thought of texting her friends had entirely escaped her mind; she was simply too excited and anxious.

Now here they were, in Ande's well-kept living room, facing each other, standing still, making no sound. Ande seemed solemn and apathetic, not at all like the Envoy standing before her now. Edna knew she used to be that way, but this had changed over time since she became an Envoy. Now, anyone this indifferent seemed almost annoying to her.

"I know why you're here," said Ande, "and you'll never succeed. You cannot kill me, for you want me alive. There's still a part of you that wants me."

"I'm not going to lie, there are times when I do still want you," Edna said, talking as if she'd known this person all her life. "But I need you gone. Your time is up. This is the day you die."

Edna was almost blindsided from a blow from Ande's armored fist. She managed to dodge it and retaliate. Ande blocked the hammer's swing, and it soon became an entanglement of steel. Edna realized this was going to be much harder than she originally thought.

Bernice hadn't travelled far from where the group had entered Laves. She wandered around the streets, peering into buildings and getting short glances at passersby. She wanted to be as unsuspicious as possible, yet it was difficult with her armor on. She was learning to not mind the awkwardness so much and even managed to put her head high with confidence in the King she was representing.

She did receive some unpleasant comments. An elf in red, modern attire jogged past her and asked, "What is that for? Do you think the city's going to be attacked?"

A creature that looked like Azarias, yet darker, half-whispered, "You don't need all those fancy things. You can get along fine without it."

One such comment actually stopped her in her tracks: "Just leave that stuff behind. You look more presentable with it off."

Bernice stopped because the voice sounded familiar. She turned to see a copy of herself with black armor and a cape. The cape looked like Bernice's flag: a yellow one with someone's face on it. After the doppelgänger not-so-subtly showed her, Bernice finally recognized the face as her own.

"I can say the same about you," Bernice said, deliberately looking at her double's armor.

"Nah, this stuff makes me look good," said the other, whose name was Ecinreb. "It makes me feel good too. You should try it on."

"No, I think I'll pass. This armor reminds me that I'm free—especially from you."

At this point, the people walking around them became fewer and fewer. Finally, it seemed they were alone.

"Did that cape by any chance use to be a flag on a weapon?" asked Bernice.

Ecinreb did not answer. She smirked instead, trying not to reveal the truth.

"Whatever happened to it?" Bernice taunted.

"Someone stole it."

"Don't tell me it was the same person who gave you that scar!"

"You can't kill me," Ecinreb said, quickly changing the subject. "Not with that thing."

"The great Vine Nazir already killed you, and I'm certainly going to try!" Bernice said as she lunged toward the doppelgänger with both hands on her spear, ready to strike. She missed, and Ecinreb was ready to counter with a kick that was unsuccessful. Bernice swung the spearhead in front of her and struck her twin in the back. The armor absorbed the blow, just as it received another one. Bernice was going to town on her, giving strike after strike.

At Laves Park, nothing could be heard but the faint rustling of blue leaves or the rapid clashing of metal. Amory and Yroma were dealing blow after blow, block after block, parry after parry. Amory wielded his sword, while Yroma threw whatever his arms and legs could deal. Yroma got a good gash across his face, but it didn't seem to faze him. Amory received a strike near the back of his knee. That did seem to faze him. Now he was limping about his opponent, circling him, trying to blitz and trick him. He succeeded only a few times.

Both men were breathing heavily now. Yroma still looked afraid yet was wearing a grin of confidence. Amory was afraid and was too tired to hide it. This doppelgänger knew how to fight and knew how to trick his opponent into thinking he had the upper hand.

There was another bout of clangs of blade and armor, all within a second of each other. Amory was trying to make his opponent expose his left side, but Yroma instead used an unknown technique to manually rip Amory's sword from his hand and wound his arm at the same time. Amory quickly limped back, but his double followed him closely. Amory finally kicked hard enough for Yroma to stop for a second. Amory took his chance and ran to a nearby tree and then drew his Dagger.

Yroma tried to lift Amory's sword but found he couldn't. Not wasting time, he charged the tree where his twin was hiding. Amory sped off from the other side of where Yroma came and threw a good punch. Yroma's hand smashed into the tree. Amory came back and gave him a beautiful sidekick to his gut—so beautiful it pushed Yroma a good two yards away from the tree.

Amory gave the charge this time and topped it off with an intimidating scream. It succeeded long enough for him to get close enough to Yroma without getting pummeled. The two clashed metal again, with Amory now using his left hand, and was dealing the apparently more painful blows. Yroma was in the Dagger's range, and he could not do much with his rival so close. He was also weakening now. The Dagger seemed to be more effective.

Finally, with a shout of triumph, Amory pierced Yroma right where the first deadly stab had been given. Yroma hunched over, tried to utter something (maybe a last word), and fell on his face, the Dagger still in his chest.

Amory rolled the corpse over and removed the Dagger, making sure to clean it quickly. He then took back his sword, and he sheathed them both. It was then that he rested a little, but only a little. He sent a text that said he had defeated his double, then bolted off. He had to find his team and see if they needed him, or at least make sure they weren't lost.

———

Ande's apartment was a lot less neat now. Due to Edna's hammer, almost everything—fragile or not—was demolished. She and Edna ended up in the bedroom, which was now the scrappiest room. The windows were broken, the nightstands in pieces, the bedframes detached, and there was now a new entryway through the wall to the kitchen.

Edna had taken a gash and a pound from Ande's spiked gauntlets, and Ande received some scars from the hammer's head and spike. Their armor had absorbed most of the blows' impacts, but the slashes from the sharp points of either weapon was a different story. Now, they were both limping toward each other to deal more hits. Edna charged faster and managed to give a strike to Ande's breastplate so powerful that it sent Ande out the window behind her. Edna waited and breathed for a bit, then went to see where her double had landed. She poked her head out the window and stopped breathing. There was no sign of Ande anywhere. There was nothing to indicate that she had even landed except for a cracked section of sidewalk.

Edna stood only for a second before she realized that Ande was probably not dead. She raced out of the room and down the stairs (the elevator would have been too slow). She stopped short when she got to the seventh floor, for there at the bottom of that flight of stairs was Ande, apparently unfazed and unscarred by the fall. No sign of blood or injury could be seen except for the small wound from Edna's spike.

"Nothing you try to do will kill me," said Ande. "And I won't kill you either. Let's stop this fighting and live in harmony. I can give you all the pleasure you want."

"Uh-huh," said Edna, blood churning in anger and zeal, "and what if we're doing something wrong, and someone sees us?"

"It doesn't matter. No one will ever have to know. And even if they do, not everyone will accept what we do. It's OK."

"It does matter," Edna said. "It matters whether or not I hurt someone, including myself! Although, some people I have to hurt, and you're one of them!"

At that, Edna turned her hammer around to where the spike was facing forward, and she darted and yelled down the stairs. Ande leaped up the stairs, and their blows met again. Edna was determined to defeat this monster, but Ande seemed stronger than before she had fallen. Every hit she took seemed to give her a slight advantage somehow.

Edna tried every move and bait to pierce that one scar, and even came close, but Ande would have none of it. Edna knew that the Dagger was the only thing that could kill the fiend, but she couldn't get an open hand; she kept having to use her hammer with both hands to fight. Each of Edna's attacks were blocked and thwarted. She was getting exhausted, and she was sure she was showing it. Her techniques were becoming more and more desperate, while Ande's were getting deadlier.

They were now on the fifth floor, as Ande had been gradually pushing Edna downstairs. Now she was swinging her hammer wildly, trying to make anything work even the slightest bit. Of course, swinging wildly didn't work. Ande was right on top of every move she made.

Suddenly, Ande's arms were locked mid-strike with Edna's hammer. Neither one could pull away. Edna took this chance and pushed her twin to the wall behind her. That hole in the armor was so close, yet Edna couldn't break her arms free to grab her Dagger, and neither could Ande get free.

"Let's make a truce," said Ande with a tired voice she was trying to hide. "Our only weapons are stuck together. Let's be friends, and we'll stick together too, not able or willing to hurt each other."

Edna knew that this was not her only weapon, and she tried desperately to get one arm remotely available without freeing her enemy too. At long last, with much wriggling on both parties, she pulled one arm free and swiftly unsheathed her Dagger. The green light began to appear, and Ande's eyes quickly widened with fear as she glanced at it. The double tried frantically to break free, but to no avail. Edna, without another word, penetrated the vital hole with the Dagger. Ande gave a small scream, then it was over. The doppelgänger fell, and that untangled the hammers. Edna took back her Dagger and left the body right there in the stairwell; she wanted nothing more to do with it.

Leona was two inches away from Anoel as her axe hooked onto Anoel's fists, then got unhooked again. Leona was trying to stay as far from her twin as possible because Anoel kept giving skillful kicks that threatened to break bones. Leona would have to kill this beast eventually, but for the moment, she just wanted to steer clear. Maybe the doppelgänger would get tired. That would be her chance.

Anoel never did get tired. The two had been all the way around the town square. In fact, they had almost gone in a complete circle. Anoel kept advancing on her double. Her techniques were certainly intimidating, and it was getting the best of Leona. Leona kept being pushed back, afraid of getting mauled by kicks she herself knew. Leona was able to block often, but she was bruised a couple of times, while Anoel hadn't been hit once.

"Just face it," said Anoel with arrogance, "I might be you, but I'm also better than you. Why don't we join together? Then we can really make a difference."

"I believe you," said Leona as she blocked another strike. "But that difference would be for the worse. I have a greater calling than that."

Anoel was now throwing her kicks more fiercely. Leona was facing an onslaught of attacks with which she could hardly keep up. Anoel skipped closer to her, and before Leona knew it, there was an armored punch coming down over her. In an instant, her axe was there to meet it, and the two warriors stood still, staring fiercely at each other's eyes. Anoel had a confident smile on her face, but then she noticed that Leona had one too. She then noticed that *she* was being pushed back now; Leona was advancing on her.

Leona had finally gotten tired of being pushed around. She was pushed around by bullies in school years ago, and now she was fighting a bully in her own image. She had had enough. She started walking forward and giving diagonal swings with her axe, temporarily forgetting about her Dagger. None of them managed to make contact with Anoel, for now she was the one backing up. Leona leapt at her a couple of times and finally gave some scars. This seemed to only give Anoel more power and confidence, though, and Anoel leapt back at her with a kick to the hip. This blow temporarily deterred Leona and made her susceptible to more punches and kicks.

Leona, being bombarded with flying fists and feet, started to close her eyes and wildly swing her axe again. It didn't seem to do much good until suddenly she realized that Anoel had stopped. All was quiet for a moment or two as Leona opened one eye to see that the tip of her axe had just barely penetrated that hole in Anoel's shoulder. Leona tried to make it go deeper, but even this thin blade was too wide. That was when Leona remembered. Anoel chuckled arrogantly, then kicked her away, and they were at it again, the doppelgänger now in full fury. She was not going to let Leona get that close again.

Leona tried her hardest to think up a new strategy to kill this monster with the one weapon she had been told to use, while fighting to keep up with all Anoel's jabs at the same time. Out of fear, she turned to her side to brace for a sidekick. Anoel kicked the sheathed Dagger, and that resulted in an explosion of green light. The evil twin winced as if in pain, and Leona puzzled at this, but only for a second. Anoel recovered and leaped toward her, but not before Leona had taken out the Dagger and positioned it. The doppelgänger leapt right into it, and it landed square in the critical scar. Anoel's face turned from one of confidence to one of absolute terror before she died.

Leona wasted no time. She cleaned her Dagger and ran in a single direction, looking for anyone from her team who might need her.

Whizz! Nylid heard and even felt arrows flashing past him. He was crouching behind a fence in the backyard of a poor and indifferent stranger. He had found this a good place to take cover as well as found small things to throw at his enemy, the archer. None of the arrows had hit him yet, but some came close, within a foot away. Nylid was utterly panicked but was determined not to get killed again.

Whump! Another stone landed quite close to Dilyn, a little too close for comfort. Dilyn was standing behind the corner of a wooden house, trying not to annoy the owners but also not blowing his cover. He grabbed another arrow from the quiver behind him and put it to the bow's string. He stepped out of hiding and aimed his weapon, only to dodge a rather large rock that landed where he was standing a second ago. This kid was really getting on his nerves. If another close call like that came, he might have to heck with it and charge at him, just to get closer.

Then, Dilyn got an idea. He would be the one who vexed his enemy out of hiding, instead of the other way around. He readied his bow again and stepped out to fire a shot that would have been frightfully close if he had fired it. He never did, as he beheld a large flying stone that met him in his right shoulder. He let the arrow fly into oblivion, himself collapsing to the ground, letting out a cry of pain. Even with the armor, that hurt!

In his groaning and wincing, he thought he heard another cry from where Nylid had been cowering. There seemed to be a scuffle over there, but Dilyn couldn't see anything or anyone. Dilyn was still lying on the ground when he heard someone call, "Dilyn, come here! I got him!"

It was Leona's voice. Dilyn smiled as he heaved himself up and jogged awkwardly to the backyard gate. When he opened it, he found Nylid face down on the ground with Leona holding onto his wrist with a judo pinning technique.

"Turn him around and finish it, Dilyn!" she said.

"Yeah, turn me around. I dare you!" groaned Nylid.

Dilyn tried to turn him over with his foot, but the beast bit his ankle, causing Dilyn to yelp and back off. Nylid immediately wiggled around and escaped Leona, who had been caught off guard by Dilyn's shout. The doppelgänger kicked, punched, twisted, and shook his way to his feet after the Envoys tried to keep him on the ground. Without a word, Nylid took off running, with two armed warriors hot on his heels.

Dilyn, not willing to waste anymore arrows, dove for his twin's ankles and wrapped his arms around them. Nylid faceplanted the ground and instantly recoiled, beating on his double to a pulp. Leona came just in time and gave him a gash on the cheek with her axe. The monster stopped short, slowly turned to face Leona with furious eyes, and lunged at her.

As Dilyn got up, he saw within a moment that Nylid had tried to attack Leona but failed. They were now several yards off.

Leona, for the moment, had him pinned in front of her, her axe at his throat.

"Do it, Dilyn! Now!" she said.

All within five seconds, Dilyn took out his Dagger, put the end of its hilt on his bow's string, and fired it. He had blinked when he let go of the string, so he worried for a split second that he missed or got the wrong person. Instead, he saw Leona standing and breathing heavily, and at her feet he saw the body of his twin with the Dagger settled directly in the breastplate's hole.

Dilyn took his Dagger, cleaned it, and put it away. Then, he and Leona journeyed back to where their group had started.

"Good shot," said Leona.

"Well, it was point-blank range, pretty much. Thanks for your help."

Leona gave him a look of well-meaning satisfaction. "You're very welcome."

———

Bernice was dealing all the strikes on her enemy and never received one in return. Bernice was fast and aggressive, and there seemed to be no stopping her—until she tried once to stab the wound with her Dagger and missed. Ecinreb instantly took advantage and began to turn the tide. Now she was throwing all the punches while Bernice did her best to block and dodge. With such a long weapon, it was hard to keep up with everything coming at her. At first, she pushed forward, determined to beat this monster who was formerly herself. After a while, though, Bernice's strength began to diminish, and she was getting pushed.

With every punch thrown by Ecinreb, she took a step back. Ecinreb noticed this and began to deal more blows faster. It came to the point where Bernice was almost jogging backwards and was really beginning to panic. At last, the doppelgänger had her pinned against the wall of a nearby shop.

"Help! Somebody, please! I'm being attacked!" cried Bernice.

"Ha!" said Ecinreb. "You attacked me! I'm just acting in self-defense. How about a truce. Then we can live together in peace."

"There is no peace with you," said Bernice angrily.

Bernice looked around. There wasn't a soul in sight. Even if there was, she wasn't sure they would care, let alone consider helping. For all she knew, they all might be against her. Bernice tried calling out again and began to wonder what this monster would do to her if she wasn't willing to join Ecinreb.

Unexpectedly a figure came from around the corner of the shop and used a long weapon to knock Ecinreb well away from her victim. Bernice instantly recognized the figure as Edna's. Bernice emitted a sigh of relief and joy.

"Thanks," she said.

"No problem," said Edna. "I got texts from the others. Everyone else's doppelgänger is dead. Yours is the last! Let's finish the mission, Bernice!"

By now, Ecinreb had recovered and was charging at them both, her cape fluttering in the wind behind her. Despite apparently being strengthened by each hit, Ecinreb was taken down by Edna and killed by Bernice.

The mission was over. The two ladies reported Ecinreb's death to the others, declaring that all five doppelgängers were finally and completely dead.

Amory texted back and said to use the Daggers to meet back up at the Center with Nazir and report to him that the mission was complete.

Since Bernice already had her Dagger out, she pointed it in front of her and quickly summoned a portal. She looked back at Edna and made sure she was ready when someone else caught Bernice's eye. She saw a familiar form a good distance behind Edna; it was a young man, maybe with blonde hair. He apparently didn't see her, as he was sauntering in the opposite direction alongside someone else who looked very similar to him. Bernice began to walk toward him as she called out: "Ambrose?"

9

GETTING EQUIPPED

Ambrose, who was wearing expensive-looking black and red armor along with a decorative sheath, turned his head to see two women—one familiar and one unfamiliar—strolling toward him and his new friend. He recognized Bernice in her orange armor, but he wasn't acquainted with the lady with the yellow armor and hammer.

"Oh, hey, Bernice," he said cheerfully. "What brings you here? Who's your friend?"

"This is Edna, another Envoy I met recently who's joining our group. Who's *your* friend?"

Ambrose smiled, as if proud of his newfound acquaintance. "This is Esorbma. He looks a lot like me, doesn't he? That's because he's my 'doppelgänger.' Ever heard of those?"

"Uh, yeah, we have," said Edna in a slight state of alarm. "We were actually here to kill our own doppelgängers because they're dangerous to us. I just helped Bernice kill hers back there." At this, she pointed to Ecinreb's corpse, and Esorbma, who Bernice noticed had no hole in his chest, coughed and subtly shrank back.

Ambrose stared at them with wide eyes and an expression of horror. "How could you do that?!" he shouted. "Doppelgängers never mean any harm to anyone! What, are you going to go around killing people with your new toys?"

"Nazir said we had to kill them because they're evil," said Bernice. "They do mean harm to us. This Esorbma intends to ruin you! He wants to take everything good about you and destroy it for the pursuit of pleasure!"

"Don't listen to that bogus," said Esorbma in a voice identical to his twin. "You're wrong, Envoys. I want to make Ambrose the best he can possibly be. I seek to help him fulfill his potential."

"There is only one who can do that," said Edna.

"Hang on," interrupted Ambrose before his double could blow a fuse. "You said something about a group. What group?"

"The five of us Nazir made into a team," Bernice said. "Amory's our leader, and there's the two of us, and Leona and Dilyn."

"Dilyn? Is he here?" Ambrose said with sudden enthusiasm.

"Around the city somewhere, yeah," said Bernice. "Why do you ask?"

"I'd like to see him again," answered Ambrose. "It's been a while."

"No, you don't," Esorbma said sternly. "You're on your own, remember? You don't need your brother here. I thought you told me you were tired of always having him around. Look, I know you miss him, but you'll both have to go your separate ways. That's part of adulthood. That's part of individuality."

"Yeah," murmured Ambrose despondently. "Welp, I guess we'd better be off. Good to see y'all again." He saw that Bernice had been on her phone for the last couple of minutes. "What are you doing?"

The text-sending sound flew from her phone. "I just texted Dilyn to come and see you."

"What?!" Esorbma cursed, his eyes appearing as though they would pop out in fury. "What'd you do that for? Meddling Envoy! Come on, Ambrose, let's hurry."

"Why?" said all three humans. The doppelgänger was silent as he grabbed Ambrose's arm and dragged him around the back corner of the block.

———

The two women sighed. "I hope Ambrose can see how ill-willed doppelgängers are *now*," huffed Bernice.

"I don't know," said Edna. "His mind could be clouded or hardened. We probably should tell Nazir if he's your friend and Dilyn's brother."

They strolled through the still-open portal, figuring Dilyn was probably already at the Center with the others and wouldn't come to where the text had been sent—it probably never got through. They were welcomed by the Vine and the other Envoys.

"What took you so long?" asked Leona.

"Well, we ran into Ambrose," said Bernice in a tone implying that something eventful had happened.

"You did?!" gasped Dilyn. "Where? Why didn't you tell me?"

"Actually we did text you, but you were probably here, so it didn't get through."

Dilyn almost swore but figured that wouldn't be smart around Nazir. "How is he?"

"He misses you," said Edna. "Quite a bit, actually. The only thing is he's found his own doppelgänger and has no intention of killing him." A despondent silence followed. "If it wasn't for that, Ambrose would probably have come with us to see you, Dilyn."

"He also had some different armor on, as if he's part of another group. I didn't ask him about it," added Bernice.

Dilyn groaned. "Nazir, can't you get him to come? Can't you redeem him before he makes an idiot of himself?"

"At this point, Ambrose would still reject me," said the Vine. "The only way for him to accept and believe in me is if he gets everything he wants, climbs to the top, and realizes it's all for nothing. Failure is what will drive him to me. So no, I can't save him before he makes an idiot of himself. He's currently too hardhearted, and he won't let me until then. But there is hope for him, and I'll keep nudging at him."

Nazir saw the Envoys' faces full of sorrow and thought. "What you did just now, Dilyn, I want you all to do constantly. You pleaded for me to save your brother. Whoever you meet who you know is not mine, I want you to plead for me to redeem them. This also applies to people who are suffering for any reason, for anyone who needs my intervention in any way. You can do this anytime and anywhere. Also, be vigilant for ways I might answer your pleas through you."

"Why is that what you want?" asked Amory.

"Because you know I can if that's what I want, and because it's a demonstration of your love for me and for those for whom you're interceding. Also, it's because you know I'm the only one who can make your hopes happen."

After a little while, Nazir changed the subject. "Now, on to your next assignment! You all did well and fought valiantly. Your doppelgängers are dead, and I am proud of each one of you! I must warn you, though, that you can somewhat bring them back to life."

"What do you mean?" asked Dilyn.

"If you start to think only for yourselves and your own pleasures and evil again, your twins can be brought back, and they will again dominate your minds like Ambrose's currently dominates his. You must focus on me and continue to bond with me. This is the only way you'll remain free. Stay with me, and my peace and my word will remain in you.

"All right, you are very close to being ready for your first large-scale mission! Before that, though, you must make adequate preparations. Your next assignment is as follows: return to Earth and obtain some stories of Envoys who have gone out into other worlds."

"There are stories about Envoys like that on Earth?" Leona asked.

"Yes," said the Vine. "We might be an elite group, but we're not exactly secretive unless necessary! Absorb these stories, and search for gatherings of Envoys throughout your cities; there are plenty. Attend these gatherings and be fed by the community and accountability you'll find there. Above all, keep coming to me. Keep these practices regular. They *will* be useful if your heart and love is in it."

The Vine continued. "After three months, on Monday, November 15th, get everything you'll need for a special quest. Get an adequate amount of food and water, along with clothes and raincoats. It'd be best to leave your phones behind; the world you'll be entering doesn't have any kind of internet. Notify your families, loved ones, and schools that you'll be away on an Envoys' mission. Some of them might not respond well, but I will soften their hearts and make sure that they let you go and give their blessing. Do you understand?"

Dilyn said, "Yes, sir."

Bernice and Edna said, "Yes, my King."

Leona and Amory said, "Yes, Father."

———

All had become quiet in the main hall of the Self-Worthy's fortress. Maewing had stepped onto an ornate podium that was decked with gold from Laves. Every creature present (which amounted to crowds larger than those at sports events on Earth) was facing her. Ambrose stood between Lisias, who was constantly in his armor, and Esorbma, who had calmed down since their encounter with those Envoys a little earlier. All three of them had eyes glowing in admiration for their leader. She had called for silence.

"We are about to embark on a new mission!" she shouted zealously. Several explosions of multilingual cheers overflowed from that enormous and quite acoustic room, Ambrose was nearly deafened and a little startled that the applause had started so soon. "This will be a major step in accomplishing our purpose: to awaken our worlds to the truth that every individual is unique and is worthy on his or her own right!"

More ovations began.

"Our target is Hertengard, the world of elves and dwarves—namely the Elven Kingdom of Liberdane. There, we will strive to replace the aging king and together promote our cause in an exponential manner!" Maewing paused to allow for more applause. Once they began to die down again, she continued, looking at Ambrose in particular.

"Once this is completed, we will be one step closer to merging all the realms of *Rôb Têbêl* and ensuring that the entire multiverse knows and lives upon the passion of the Self-Worthy! This is now possible because the Sword of *Chârâsh* is presently in our midst! Mr. Ambrose Brandt, could you lift up your Sword for us?"

Ambrose barely heard the applause, which was mixed with gasps of amazement, that was crowding him. He suddenly felt very timid and flushed. He was also confused; hadn't Maewing said not to let anybody see this Sword? Maybe she meant anybody outside the Self-Worthy. That made sense.

Hesitantly, Ambrose pulled the Sword from his ornate, black sheath. First there was silence, then the loudest cheers and claps that Ambrose had ever heard. Lisias, Esorbma, and numerous others patted him on the back and commended him. He no longer felt timid but now important upon receiving all this attention and favor. Perhaps this was what the Self-Worthy was all about.

Ambrose started getting mobbed with questions on how it was possible for him to get this treasure, but before he could get his bearings and answer, Maewing continued.

"Now, I'm sure Mr. Brandt will be happy to answer all your questions another time, but now is the time for adequate training. Our focus must be on acquiring Liberdane, one of the most prominent nations in the elven world. In preparation, I recommend that you all obtain some sort of armor and weapons. We don't have enough in the armory to supply everybody, so we will need to obtain some from other places throughout Ourrance. All of this will likely take a couple of months. Let's be ready sooner. Let's go!"

And with that, the crowds became a chaotic mass of creatures trying to get to a hundred different places at once. Ambrose found himself being led by his twin down a couple of smaller hallways to what he said was the armory. Ambrose wasn't cheering or hollering like everyone else; he was deep in thought over what he had been told.

So, she wants to use this Sword to merge the multiverse and make the Self-Worthy rule it? he thought. *Strange, yet effective enough, I'd say. I wonder what Nazir would have to say about this.* Ambrose grinned to himself at this humorous notion.

PART III

THE MISSION

10

JOURNEYS
IN THE STORM

M aewing, clad in her silver and white armor, proudly and erectly led a multitude of diverse troops through her castle walls. She seemed so enthusiastic that her black wings frequently flapped as if she would take off then and there. In both her hands she held swords, one of which was thin and pointed like a fencer's rapier, and the other had a double-edged blade on either end of the handle. In addition to all her equipment, she wore one of the widest smiles she had ever worn.

Ambrose marched directly behind her in the front of the immense crowd of armed creatures. Beside him strode an elf named Ives, who was to be their guide since Hertengard was his home world. Because Ambrose possessed the Sword of *Chârâsh* and he had done so well in his brief combat training, Maewing had already promoted him to captain. Along with the new title, Ambrose had received a miniature crossbow for his wrist and an intricate golden shield that blinded enemies in the sunlight. He wore these now, along with his beautiful cutlass and red armor.

The Self-Worthy armies halted at the open gate of the fortress. Their queen turned stately around and looked Ambrose in the eyes with the smile of a warrior and a friend.

"Ambrose," she said, "since you have used the Sword of *Chârâsh*, tell me what it's like to use it and exactly how you got here."

Ambrose told her how he had used the Sword to summon a portal and how upon entering it, he had found himself in an underground place with passages to each world's individual portal.

Maewing's smile grew even wider. "So, the legends are true. Possessors of the Sword travel underground between the realms. We will need to march in single file, then. Do you know where the portal to Hertengard is?"

"No, ma'am, I don't. I pretty much only know how to get here and back to Earth."

"That's all right," said Maewing. She then called out, "Lisias!"

The faun wormed his way through the soldiers and stood at attention before his leader. "Yes, your majesty?"

"For the last time, stop calling me that. I am equal to you! Will you please go in front with Ambrose, Ives, and me to find Hertengard?"

"It would be my utmost and sincere pleasure," said Lisias, who caught himself bowing.

"Lisias has been to multiple worlds before," Maewing explained to Ambrose. "He is a former Envoy of Nazir."

"Ah, so you've heard of Nazir!" said Ambrose. "What do you think of him?"

"I don't doubt his existence," said Maewing, "but I've heard that he remains in one location, while every other creature, including his Envoys, are everywhere else. He simply strikes me as a distant and apathetic being. Also, his Envoys say that he is the only one who can make anyone worthy, and we know that's not true!"

"So you don't like him, then?" asked Ambrose.

Maewing's grin waned a little bit. "I like him enough. He has very upright views and values, and I respect that. It's just that some of his views conflict with mine, and those views forbid us to be friends. At any rate, the time has now come! Captain Brandt, unsheathe your Sword and take us to Hertengard!"

Ambrose pointed the immortal weapon forward, trembling with excitement and nervousness and bracing himself for the Sword's jolt when it shot forth its jade beam. In doing so, he thought, *It's clear now that I cannot choose both the Self-Worthy and the Envoys. For now, I'll stick with these guys because I don't know what they'd do to me if I left them now. But I wonder, why can't someone get Maewing and Nazir to compromise and join forces? Then nothing could stop us in our quest to show fulfillment to others! Maybe I could be the one to unite the Self-Worthy and the Envoys....*

Leona, Edna, Dilyn, Bernice, and Amory, wearing armor as well as backpacks full of food, water, and other necessities, strode proudly and excitedly into the Center, where Nazir was waiting for them, looking the same as he had when they had first seen him. To his left erectly stood Azarias, holding some sort of bundles of clothing with both arms. One bundle was scarlet and silver, and the other indigo and crimson.

"Welcome back, my children!" said Nazir in his same delighted, yet solemn tone.

"Hello, Father!" Amory said, who was also quite cheerful.

"Hey, Azarias!" said Leona. "What are you doing here?"

"Nazir summoned me to give you these two garments and sets of armor," said the cherub majestically. "I've been waiting over seven decades to construct these and have been anticipating the time of their predestined wearers to come. Now, it finally has."

"Do your families know you're here?" asked Nazir.

"My mom was skeptical at first, but she's warmed up to the idea," said Leona.

"My parents did *not* approve of me going at first," said Bernice, "but after they saw how serious I was, they said I could. I still don't know if they like this idea, but they're letting me go, as long as I promise to return safely."

"Mine said pretty much the same thing," Dilyn said.

"Mine were actually excited that I go!" said Edna. "They actually wished it was sooner, but I reminded them that I wasn't ready until now."

Amory didn't answer and was thankful he didn't have to.

"It is time for your first quest to begin," said Nazir more earnestly. "Pay very close attention, my children. I am sending you to Hertengard, the world where elves and dwarves live. That world is in serious danger because one of its mightiest nations, Liberdane, is crumbling under the rule of a corrupt tyrant. If Liberdane falls, all Hertengard will eventually collapse as well, and any connection to me will be lost. That cannot happen. Therefore, I am sending you five into Liberdane to reestablish my rule there. You are to bring these two sets of armor to a couple of orphaned elves. It is through them and through you that I intend to make myself better known there. If all else fails, I want you to teach these two about me, as they are not Envoys."

"That seems like a lot on the line for only five people who have only been with you for a few months," said Amory.

"All the better," Nazir replied. "More people see and come to me when they know beyond a shadow of a doubt that I was working there. Without me, it is impossible for five humans and two lonely elves to make the difference you are meant to make there. But with me, you will accomplish the impossible. When you are most vulnerable, that's where I am shown the most . . . if you let me.

"Amory and Dilyn, each of you take a set of armor, and do not lose either of them. They are not Envoys' armor, but the recipients will need them nonetheless for defense. Lead them to me. Then, they will become Envoys and receive their badges and true armor. When you go through the portal directly to my right and find yourselves on the edge of Liberdane, go straight in the direction you're put in. If you have any questions at all, you can always use your Daggers and come to me, but you will not be able to go to any other world until your mission is completed. Now, are you ready for the first of many adventures of your lives?"

"Yes!" all five exclaimed.

"Then go and bring me to the two elves and to all of Liberdane!"

The troop of five, feeling more stoked than they had ever before been, marched through the portal to Hertengard.

Azarias dared to shuffle closer to Nazir. "I know that you can do the impossible, my Liege, but these Envoys are not ready for this assignment. They have not even been trained by other Envoys! They will fail!"

"They might, Azarias," said the Vine, "but no other Envoys in *Rôb Têbêl* are suited for this task. They might not seem as prepared as some others might be, but they are. I equipped them with all they need to accomplish this task. These five have a combination of talents that no other group has and therefore are the best choice for the conquest of Liberdane. I, through them, must retain and restore my kingdom there. Even if they do fail, be reminded, Azarias, that I never do."

"One last thing, my King. With great hesitance, I obeyed your command to let Dilyn's brother take the multiversal Sword. May I ask why you let him steal it?"

"Because that is how this mission, and several others in the future, can be accomplished. The Self-Worthy do not know me and do not operate on all my standards. There will be justice for Ambrose's theft, but this will lead to my kingdom's advancement. Do you trust my judgement, Azarias?"

"Of course I trust you, as I always have! And if this is for the sake of your kingdom and your name, then I will certainly comply!"

The Envoys gazed at their new surroundings. It was gray and destitute everywhere. Blond, short grass blanketed the mostly flat landscape, dotted here and there with gray, withered, leafless trees. The air was warm, humid, and still. Behind them was a gray brick wall about eight feet high with no windows or gates. The setting sun was trying desperately to shine through the clouds that thickly bordered every inch of the atmosphere, coating the entire sky in an eerie orange. Frequent flashes of blue lightning briefly took the Envoys' minds off the constantly rolling thunder.

"What the heck happened to this place?" thought Leona aloud.

"Life must not have been prosperous here for several years," Dilyn said.

"Perhaps that's part of what we're meant to fix," said Amory with a new, strange gleam in his eye. "Straight forward, friends, as our King specified."

"Into *that*?" Edna said, pointing with concern toward a distant forest, which looked as if it was getting tortured by rain and possibly hail. Above the forest hovered a thick mass of gray clouds which seemed to be rotating. "I lived in Tornado Alley for a time," Edna continued. "That cloud looks like it could become a twister by the time we get there. Are you sure Nazir doesn't want us to wait for the storm to pass?"

"I can see the cloud and the rain moving in this direction," Bernice said. "Whether we wait or stay, we're going to get hit!"

"It seems that the best option would be to go toward the storm; it's already coming toward us anyway! Besides, if we wait, the storm and potential tornado would be worse here than it would be if we were further ahead."

"We will go forward," said Amory. "Put on your coats, and cover the food and extra armor. One way or another, things are going to get wet!"

Maewing excitedly led her armies along the Liberdane countryside. Upon entering the realm, the Self-Worthy went a tad to the right (east, according to Ives's map) and saw nothing but remote, gray forests and mountains, plus the dead plains through which they were marching. Black, rumbling clouds loomed ahead of their path, and mighty winds chilled their bones.

"Where exactly are we headed?" asked Ambrose, marching between Ives and Lisias.

"To Diamond Culet, the castle of King Ever, who is the elven ruler of Liberdane," said Maewing, whose tone seemed slightly solemn. "Anyone who has been here knows that he acts more like a totalitarian, ousting all his dukes and earls by one means or another and absorbing all power for himself. He extorts his people, leaving them with barely anything to survive. Our mission is to overthrow him and replace his rule with our own. Our standards of power are much stricter and more selfless. The elves and dwarves who live here will very likely welcome any other rulers besides Ever, and they will be much more receptive to the message we have for them. We are to give their lives purpose and meaning!"

"I thought they could do that themselves," Ambrose said.

"Well, they can . . . if they have the freedom to. Ever's only living for himself and no one else. He's the only one here who possesses the liberty to do as he wishes. He even divorced his wife, Queen Gwenore, after a century of marriage simply because he had gotten tired of her! Once Ever's off the throne, the people will have the freedom to be worthy on their own right. Do you understand now, Captain Brandt?"

"Yes, I do."

Just then, the armies found themselves getting pelted by a rapidly advancing downpour. Several groans and nonhuman bellows were heard, some from Ambrose.

"Courage, comrades!" called Maewing. "We continue forward! The people of Liberdane are depending on our persistence!"

The squadrons trudged on, barely able to see where they were going, as the rain was gushing over their hoods into their faces. Their marching was much less organized, and those with fur began to lag. Maewing herself seemed undaunted by the storm, even though her strides were far from straight.

Ambrose gripped the Sword much tighter, fearing it might get blown away. He certainly did not want to part with it now; it seemed to contribute greatly to his life's meaning. More than once, he was tempted to pretend to stagger away from the armies and escape Hertengard and go back safely to Ourrance, or even to Earth. He truly began to miss his parents, his brother, and those he called friends. But he had new friends now, friends he would fight alongside, friends who admired him even more than those mortal humans back in Craghill.

For a split second, Ambrose thought he saw something of a silo or tower to his right through the wall of rain. "Where are we?" he called at the top of his lungs.

"Farm country," shouted Ives in a rugged elvish accent. "We'll pass many farms along our journey . . . hopefully. This is one of the largest, yet still unsuccessful estates."

Ambrose didn't quite hear everything Ives said because of the downpour for one thing, and for another, because he and several others caught a glimpse of a rotating cloud straight before them, less than a mile away. It wasn't long before soldiers in numerous languages started calling out, "Tornado! Tornado!"

Indeed, it was a tornado, and it was massive. Ambrose could hardly see either end of it; he only saw the bulge in front of them. Before Maewing could give any commands, she was swept up and around by the cyclone. As about a third of the armies (all in the back of the procession) scattered frantically, most of the troops, including Ambrose, found themselves flying midair by an uncontrollable force. Ambrose braced as he splashed through the outer lining of the whirlwind, then dared to open his eyes.

It was still raining inside the tornado, but the raindrops were going sideways with the winds. There was plenty of crashing and screaming about. Ambrose nearly ran into several soldiers or other objects, such as a portion of a makeshift fence, a large stone, and a scrawny version of what was similar to a goat. He occasionally felt something zoom above or below him and soon discovered that it was Maewing, flying with her tremendous wings, attempting to avoid any oncoming projectiles. It seemed like she was struggling to do so.

Before Ambrose could see or be amazed anymore, he saw that he was being flung by the winds to the tornado's border again. He burst into the outside world—still in midair—and for a brief moment saw the wooden top of the silo. He crashed through the roof and landed shortly after, drifting out of consciousness.

The Envoys were several miles west of the Self-Worthy, but they were caught in the same tempest. They had been soaked with rain within the first ten minutes of entering the storm, and now their helmets were being pelted by hail. That and the constantly shrieking winds made it very difficult to remain on the straight path. They soon found themselves in a loose forest, with unidentifiable trees swaying dangerously above them.

"Maybe we should take shelter somewhere!" cried Dilyn, struggling to keep the extra armor in his grip. "Is there a cave or a lodge nearby?"

His voice was barely audible to himself, let alone anyone else. They simply trudged on, trusting that Nazir had given the right path to tread and trusting that Amory was actually going on that path. They could see almost nothing before them through the wall of rain, though it seemed to get cloudier and windier than before. All too late, Amory saw ahead of them a wide wall of water, as if it was a small tidal wave on the shore.

Before he could tell the others to run, he turned and saw Edna and Leona getting blown by a fierce gust into an enormous, distant tree. As that happened, another tree collapsed near Bernice. Amory didn't see what the result was, for a lightning bolt had struck the ground very near Dilyn and briefly blinded him with a small, short-lived explosion. After recovering his sight, Amory looked in vain for his team and beheld the rapidly advancing wall of gray and blue, now only a few yards from him.

"Nazir, why?" he cried and was blown off the ground by the wave.

Ambrose awakened suddenly, groaning under a substantial headache. He sat up and looked around. A beam of hazy light poked through a hole in the silo's ceiling, which was a few feet above him. The entire structure, inside and out, seemed to be made of thin, gray wood. For a few moments, Ambrose was afraid to move lest he fall through the floor. He finally got up and came to the edge of a staircase that spiraled around the empty center. He discovered that there were at least a dozen floors below him.

"So, you escaped all right too," came an accented groan. Ambrose twirled to find Ives and a woman standing—yet hunched over—near the beam of light.

"I guess so," said Ambrose. "A few unforgettable bruises, but beyond that, I'm not injured. You?"

"We're OK," said the woman in a high voice. "More relieved than anything else."

"Yes, hopefully the rest of the armies are of the same condition," said Ives.

The trio slowly treaded down the stairs. Their descension was careful not to disturb their wounds and to ensure the wood wouldn't give way. After what seemed like several dark hours, they came out to find multiple hundreds of hobbling troops spread out across the field as far as the eye could see—and perhaps even further. Creatures of all kinds were limping about to find weapons they'd dropped or friends they'd lost. The female trooper joined them in the searches.

Ambrose noticed that the ground was much firmer than he expected after a storm like the one last night. He also noted to himself that light gray clouds still loomed, but the white sun was allowed to shine more brightly. He made a bewildered face at Ives.

"This is all part of the ancient curse of Hertengard," said the elf, breaking the dismal silence. "Disastrous storms appear all too frequently, yet the ground almost instantly returns to being unplowable. Many farms and communities have gone destitute because of this thousand-year-old curse."

"What caused such a curse?" Ambrose asked.

Before Ives could reply, a disturbance arose from the soldiers on their right. They limped toward the crowd of beings, some of whom were crying in anguish and others hushed with horror. Four minotaurs were carrying a large, makeshift stretcher made of a thick, ragged canvas tied to two wooden poles. On the stretcher, to the dismay of all, was Maewing.

"My lady, what happened?!" Ives cried.

Maewing struggled to speak in groans. "In the tornado, I crashed into a large stone, breaking one of my wings, then dropped with nothing to break my fall. Upon impact, I might have broken two or three legs. I'll live, don't worry about that, but I am calling off the mission. I cannot call my friends to do something I am unable or unwilling to do myself. We will need to recover for a month or two before attempting to take Liberdane again, and next time, we will ensure the weather is relatively clear first!"

"Begging your pardon, ma'am," said Ambrose, "but why do we need to cancel the mission? Not everyone is injured. I still see many able soldiers who would be more than willing to conquer King Ever for you!"

"I won't be with you," said Maewing. "A leader must go to battle with his or her troops."

"I'll be the leader for you then! I know I'm only a captain, so send everyone who is above my rank with you and the injured back to Ourrance, and I will take Liberdane!"

"It makes sense to me," said Esorbma, who approached the group without any apparent injury or scar. "Besides, Ever is evidently soon to die, and if we aren't here when that happens, someone else will take his place as king."

"Of course, it makes sense to you," said Maewing. "You're his double. All you want is his exaltation and fulfilled desires."

"I don't want to take Ever's place," Ambrose said, "I only want to overtake him before someone else does. As soon as we do, I'll report back to you, so you can be the new ruler."

"I agree with the lad," Ives said. "This could be our only opportunity to take Hertengard. We may not have the luxury of waiting for another chance. I'll stay with him and guide him, my lady. Nothing will go awry."

The Self-Worthy leader thought for an agonizingly long moment. The minotaurs carrying her started to fidget, not wanting to stand still much longer. Finally she gave an answer.

"All right, Captain Brandt, you have my consent. Take whoever is uninjured and not carrying someone who is injured, regardless of rank, and follow Ives to Diamond Culet and conquer Liberdane. Please make a portal for us so we can go home and recover as soon as possible."

The large, green portal was created, and the minotaurs marched off, leading a developing procession back in the direction from which they had come. Ambrose thought he saw Lisias among the injured, being supported by a fellow faun, but he couldn't get to him through the immense horde.

Maewing called back to Ambrose and Ives as they left. "You might come across the tower where Queen Gwenore lives. It might be good to pay her a visit first." She said something else, but they did not hear her as she and her carriers strolled through the portal and vanished.

The captain and the elven guide gathered the remaining troops, which was sadly less than a third of the original amount. Fortunately the new amount was still quite large, numbering to about ten thousand. One of them approached Ives and indeed looked very much like Ives.

"Is that your doppelgänger?" Ambrose exclaimed. "How many of you guys have one?"

"I think we all do," said Ives. "This is Sevi!"

"Does Maewing have one, and if so, where is she?"

3

THE CONNECTOR
OF WORLDS

As our heroes continued walking through the portal, it became clear that they were not dead. They didn't want to stop walking, lest they somehow get vaporized. After a few seconds, they began to notice that there was an end to the portal—another side. The students went closer to the end, awestruck when they finally came out.

They were now in a new place, and it was definitely not on Earth. It seemed that they were inside a spherical object, except the round walls displayed an array of space, like a beautiful night sky above, around, and below them. They were immediately struck with a powerful, rich, savory smell. It smelled like a wonderful piece of meat, accompanied by a subtle sweet aroma that blended perfectly with the meaty smell. The sphere they were in was not at all cramped; there were several square feet of room. On select places in the walls were several other portals. At a distance, the visitors looked inside some of them and saw only pure white. They all assumed (with some disbelief) that behind the white were different worlds.

"Cool!" said Ambrose. "Let's explore these places!"

"Wait," Bernice said, "what about the one we just left?"

They looked back at the portal they had come through. It was still showing the same spot they had come from on Earth. All of a sudden, the scene in the portal began to change. The kids all watched with hidden fear as the scene changed from a dark, mysterious cavern to one of white like the others.

The five looked forward again. They noticed that in the center of the sphere was a rather large plant. It was green everywhere, except in its veins, which were pure white. They realized that the smell they were absorbing was coming from this plant. It had multiple bulky branches extending from its stem, which was as thick and tall as a tree trunk. Some branches, as the children noticed, stopped growing in random places, with large, open leaves on the ends. Others stretched all the way along the walls toward and through all the portals. The plant, as the kids got a closer look, appeared more like a vine. To their great surprise, they heard a voice arise from the vine.

"Welcome!"

The voice was male and sounded like a human's. It was very quiet, though they figured it could be very loud if need be. His tone sounded solemn and friendly at the same time. It took a minute before Amory finally spoke up.

"U-h, hi. You can talk?" As shaky as Amory's words were, his thoughts were shuddered to the core and bounced every which way. New ideas, theories, possibilities, and logics bloomed in his head, as well as in the other four heads present.

The vine chuckled. "Yes. I know you're not used to hearing plants talk, so this is quite a surprise for you. There are many more surprises in store, though. You all have much to learn and see."

"You *know*?" Ambrose said. "Have you been watching us?"

"Yes, Ambrose," said the vine. The fact that he knew Ambrose's name led the kids to believe him. "I am Nazir, and you have just entered the center of *Rôb Têbêl*, the multitude of worlds."

11

THE CURSE
OF HERTENGARD

A rgh!" uttered Dilyn as he awakened with a jump. He found
himself soaked and breathing heavily, lying amidst a bed
of interwoven, bare branches suspended in a tree. Feeling the
soreness envelope his body, he groaned as he attempted to sit
up, succeeding in his second try. He glanced cautiously below
him, relieved that the ground wasn't too far—only about four
feet. A gleam caught his eye, and Dilyn saw his bow caught
in an overhead branch. He wiggled it out and then checked
the rest of his equipment. All his armor and his Dagger were
still on him, and his quiver still had some arrows. Grateful, he
began his careful descent.

He plopped to the ground, rather shocked that it was as
dry as it was. The dirt, shrubs, and trees around him were barren
and dry, as if there had been no storm at all. He seemed to be
the only thing in that spacious forest that was wet. Near him lay
several tall, fallen trees, and beside one stood Bernice.

"You OK?" she asked.

"I will be," groaned Dilyn. "What the heck happened?"

"I think a lightning bolt knocked you out, from what I could tell, and a ginormous wave of water scattered us," Bernice said.

Dilyn looked puzzled.

"Don't you remember the storm and the lightning burst?" Bernice asked.

Dilyn pondered for a moment. "No. Was it bad?"

"Bad?!" Bernice stepped back in surprise and concern. "It was terrible! It pretty much wiped us all out! Are you sure you're OK? Are you suffering from amnesia or something?"

"Only concerning the storm, probably. I remember our mission and that Azarias gave Amory and me the . . . oh, crud! Where's the extra armor he gave us?!"

Just then, they heard a crackling in the leafless tree above Dilyn. After a moment or two, the armor he had been carrying dropped onto the ground, and the garment followed, giving a splat. Soon afterward, Edna and Leona managed to get to the ground from that tree after climbing through endless, spiky branches.

"We found ourselves and the equipment lying on the thicker branches when we woke up," said Leona. "Boy, that storm did wonders!"

"Where's Amory?" Bernice asked, looking about herself.

After several panicked moments of searching and calling, the Envoys heard Amory call back, several yards away. He came hobbling toward them, still hanging onto his extra set of armor.

"There you are!" he gasped. "Thank goodness! Nazir said I'd run into you soon."

"Wait, what?" asked Edna. "How did you find him? Don't tell me you used your Dagger! Are you trying to ditch us or something?"

Edna's last remark was somewhat sarcastic, but Amory thought otherwise.

"I awakened near the edge of the forest, where we had first come in. I called out constantly for you guys, but I didn't hear any reply. I became so upset and desperate that I decided to ask Nazir what to do, since he said we could before we left. He didn't seem mad or to suspect that I was deserting. He just maintained his same kind, solemn tone.

"I told him all about the storm and how we seemed to have botched the mission within a day. He said we hadn't failed, and he was proud of me for turning to him for help instead of trying something on my own. Honestly I don't know what else I'd have done. I don't know this world at all!

"Anyway, he gave me directions to keep us on course. He said we never got off course, but we were simply set back. The direction I went to find you is the same direction we need to take now, which Nazir said was north."

"OK, good," Bernice said. "When I woke up, I had no idea where we were or what direction to go. Good call."

"Unfortunately," added Dilyn, "I lost my pack of food and clothes. What I'm wearing now is all that's left."

Leona and Edna realized that they also lost theirs. "Should we look back in the tree we were blown into?" asked Leona.

"No," Amory said rather firmly. "Nazir wants us to be on the move now. He said we can't tarry any longer. He'll ensure that we keep going as long as we actually are going. Bernice and I will share what necessities we have left. We'd better get on the move."

Begrudgingly the team began their trek again, with substantially less zeal than when they had started the first time.

For a few hours, they hardly heard anything. The forest was utterly silent, except for the occasional scurrying of a small, otherworldly creature. They were too quick for the Envoys to see what they were. At one point, Edna thought she saw a rabbit sprint into a gray log, but Dilyn said it was too small and too red to be a rabbit. What animals they did see were all scrawny, apparently desperate for any water, which the trees and ground would not spare.

Suddenly, a male scream filled the humid, windless air. It sounded frantic, as if its owner was fighting for his life. Before his second cry was heard, the Envoys darted to its source, which was a tad to their right, down a shallow ridge whose edge blocked their view of the evident skirmish.

Amory, Leona, and Edna, who were the quickest runners, leaped over the ridge's edge first. Before Bernice and Dilyn could, they heard another scream, this time female. The pair looked to their left and, to their horror and awe, beheld a giant figure, reaching over seven feet in height. It was clad in dark gray, odd armor, yet was otherwise unarmed. Its round, intimidating helmet overshadowed its face, except for the protruding nose.

The being was grunting horribly, stepping and spinning as fast as it could in that heavy armor. It was trying to catch a more human-sized creature, apparently the source of the female scream. She was so quickly evading the fiend's attempts to grab her that it was difficult for Dilyn and Bernice to see her well. All they could tell was that she was wearing very old clothes and had long, brown hair.

Utterly terrified, the woman darted around trees as well as the armed creature's legs and grabbing hands. "Please, let me go!" she cried. "I've done nothing to offend you or the king! I beg you, do not take me to *him*!"

The beast ignored her plea. "Come here, impossible child! I'll take you to his majesty if it kills me!"

The woman found a chance to run from the fiend's grasp. Knowing she couldn't outrun him, she made an attempt at climbing a distant tree near the Envoys. Before she could reach a cloud of branches, though, the soldier caught her by the neck and took her from the tree. Evidently not choking, the woman flailed her limbs at her catcher, failing to harm him. Without warning, the fiend yelped and writhed back, letting go of her. She dropped to the ground, and then he did, an arrow lodged in his neck.

The woman stood up instantly and started sprinting from her dead hunter, not desiring to ensure he was dead. Constantly looking over her shoulder at him, she bumped into Dilyn and Bernice, who didn't want to lose her. Panting, she looked frantically about herself for a moment, then settled down enough to take a longer look at the armored pair standing before her.

"You fired that arrow?" she asked Dilyn, pointing at his bow.

"Yes. Are you—"

"My thanks are yours," she interrupted. "Where is he? Did you see him at all?"

The other three Envoys came running, and with them a man who looked very much like the woman, save his long, thin beard and slightly bulkier build.

"Fyn!" the man cried. He was also panting.

"Eoin!" said the woman, and the pair hugged tightly, yet briefly.

Now that they were standing somewhat still, the Envoys could survey them better. Both were wearing tattered yet quite adequate gray and brown garments. Their shoes, if they weren't sandals originally, were sandals now: a few strips of leather wrung over a rather flat sole. They both were quite skinny and had brown hair. Her hair was darker and wavier and fell to her knees, and his was lighter and straighter and fell to his waist. The Envoys could also tell now that they were elves.

The duo turned to their rescuers, a look of skeptical curiosity filling the male elf's face. "Who are you, from whence have you come, and why have you come at all?" he asked.

Amory stepped forward. "We are Envoys of Nazir, the Great Vine and the King of the multiverse. Nazir sent us from another world to come and help you and your world."

The elven couple simply stared with eyebrows furrowed, mouths shut, and heads tilted.

"I'm Amory, and this is Bernice, Dilyn, Leona, and Edna. We all come from a world called Earth."

"My name is Eoin, and this is the closest and most beautiful companion I could hope to have: Fynballa." Eoin bowed as he said this, and a slight curtsy was given by Fynballa, who was smirking at her flatterer.

"You're married?" asked Leona.

"Nay," said Fynballa matter-of-factly. "We have held the hope of being wed for almost thirty years but have never had the opportunity, what with being on the run."

"Wait, how old are you?" asked Dilyn. "You both look like you're in your twenties. And why are you running away? What are you running from?"

"We constantly evade the legions of King Ever, Liberdane's ruler," said Fynballa. "He is continuously fortifying his castle and making pleasure for himself at the expense of his slaves. He takes anyone he can spare to build walls or make life easier and better for himself. Since Eoin and I possess no consistent occupation, his majesty has attempted to enslave us multiple times, but we have always escaped the clutches of his troops. We have been running for so long that we lost count of our ages. I believe we are around seventy years of age."

"Wow!" said Leona. "You sure look good for your age!"

"Actually I would say we do not," Eoin said. "Humans, I hear, only live for approximately a century, correct? Elves usually live eight or ten times as long. I would say we appear rather slovenly . . . at least I do."

"I'd say you both look lovely," Bernice said.

"That is the curious thing, though," added Fynballa, "we still look elven. However, the king, his family, his armies and court, and everyone who supports him appear much differently. They take on the form of goblins and hobgoblins, such as the soldiers you just killed. It is a part of the Curse of Hertengard."

"Curse? What curse?" asked Edna skeptically.

Eoin answered, "Since shortly after the world's beginning, Hertengard has been under a certain curse that can never be lifted. I do not recall how it is specifically described, but in a sense, it says that the state of each nation depends on the character of its rulers to the utmost degree. If the king and queen are good, then the land flourishes, being beautiful and bountiful. However, if they are evil, then the land unnaturally becomes barren and dry, even after tempests such as that of last night. In addition, the rulers themselves, along with anyone who supports them, lose their physical glory and transform into goblins. They actually do not appear as frightening as they do humorous."

"Well, all evidence indicates that Liberdane's under an evil ruler," said Dilyn, looking at the leafless trees and gray clouds. "How did he come to power? Did he kill or conquer his way to the throne, or did he do something politically or maritally illegal?"

"Nay," said Fynballa. "The crown is his by every right. He abided by every law until his coronation, and even now he does, though he has drastically twisted those laws."

"Perhaps lifting the curse is what Nazir sent us to do," Bernice said to Amory.

"Who is this Nazir of whom you speak?" asked Eoin with an even more curious expression.

"Nazir is a giant Vine who lives in the center of the multiverse," began Amory. "He created each and every world, and his branches go into each one, showing that he has a presence in each world. He is the King of the entire multiverse, and he is good. Actually he's the epitome and origin of good! He loves us and wants us to turn from our evil nature and toward him."

"Our evil nature?" asked Fynballa.

"Yes," said Leona. "Even though he made us to love him and live in his goodness and love, we are consumed by our own pride and do things our own way. Since he's the essence of good, he cannot allow evil to live with him, so we're justly doomed to an eternal death."

"But Nazir made a way to fix that!" added Edna. "He made it to where all we have to do to forsake our evil is to accept and believe in his power of redemption and authority as King! If we do, then he makes us clean, and he makes us his Envoys, who are meant to give this story to everyone in the multiverse at his leading . . . and to make more Envoys."

A long, agonizing silence followed. Amory was about to add something, but Eoin suddenly chuckled. "I see, you are another of those movements that have ravaged our nation before! You are a special society, looking only to make more members!"

"Stop, Eoin," said Fynballa, who then turned to the Envoys. "Listen, you five are of the kindest people we have met in a long while, and you saved us both from slavery, of which both of us are substantially grateful. This Nazir sounds like everything for which we have ever hoped, but that is exactly why I hesitate; he sounds too good to be true."

"Would you like to meet him?" asked Amory. "We can arrange that immediately!"

"Truly?" asked Fynballa.

"No, thank you," Eoin cut in. "If you desire to rescue Liberdane from turmoil, can you not do it without implementing your superstitions?"

"Superstitions?!" said Leona. "Listen, you can call Nazir what you want, but the fact is that he's real! I've seen him! I've heard him and touched him and even smelled him!"

"And has he seen, heard, and touched you as well?"

"Of course!"

"Wait, wait," called Amory, stepping between Eoin and Leona. "We can settle this a different way." He turned to the elves. "It will be dark in a few hours, and our rations are low. Would you like to have a quick lunch with us? And afterward, is there a town or city nearby?"

"Yes," Eoin said. "There lies a village named Growan a decent distance west. That is where Fyn and I were headed before being ambushed. You are welcome to walk with us there if you promise to not speak of Nazir for the duration of the trek. We should arrive by dusk, and yes, we would be pleased to eat with you now, as we have not put food nor drink in our mouths since yesterday."

Amory nodded, not willing to verbally give such a promise as to not mention his King, but the nod seemed to satisfy the elves. Everyone sat down on the dead grass, and Bernice and Amory distributed all they had left: seven sandwiches. Not much conversation occurred during that quick meal, except for the elves, between occasional cautious glances around them, sharing the differences between elven and human food. Now, the people of Liberdane lived off mainly cheese and the worst of meats (the best was all mandatory tribute to the king), while the livestock lived off any plants that managed to survive until harvest.

"You would have enjoyed the lush Liberdane," said Fynballa. "I don't remember what it was like, since it has been so long, but we do hear descriptions from locals every so often. They say that some trees have crystal leaves and produce edible, juicy gems as fruit. That is merely a scent of how luscious the land was."

Eoin grinned. "Legend also has it that in the olden days of intense warfare, fairies—male and female—served as elite warriors for Liberdane. Sadly, that fantastical race is all but extinct now. My favorite tales, however, were of Wybirt the Zealous, whose sword's blade was a white-hot flame!"

Everyone smiled upon hearing how Liberdane was supposed to be and what it would hopefully return to being.

After everyone was finished, which only took about ten minutes, the elven pair arose and began strolling and beckoned the Envoys to follow.

They had not gone more than twenty paces when Eoin looked down and suddenly cried, "Fyn, your shoes! They are close to falling apart! Why did I not notice sooner?"

"They continue to suit me tolerably, Eoin. Even if they do become unmendable, I would fare well without them."

"No, you would not. The terrain is too rough. Take my shoes. I would fare much better."

"Eoin, this is not a debate. I am fine."

"I would not be if I knew you would potentially be more easily caught!"

"Actually," interrupted Dilyn, producing the crimson set of clothes and armor, "you won't need to trade anything. Naz—I mean, we—were sent with these garments and equipment and were told to give them to the first elves we meet. These are for you."

Dilyn and Amory gave the intrigued couple their gifts. Fynballa got the smaller, indigo set while Eoin got the crimson one. They immediately put on the new garments over the old ones. The Envoys wondered why they didn't simply dispose of the old clothes, but none said anything.

"Remarkable!" Fynballa said. "They fit perfectly!"

"Aren't you going to put on the armor too?" asked Edna.

Eoin gave her a somber glance. "We have been doing our best to avoid battle with his majesty. We are not political activists, nor are we about to become that. Evil though he is, Ever remains our authority. You may present that armor to another, more zealous pair. Come, Growan is this way."

The newly clothed elves led on, and Amory and Dilyn picked up the apparatus again and brought up the rear. They both were quite concerned over how things were turning out. For a long while, no one spoke, until Bernice finally said, "How long have you two known each other?"

"Since early childhood," said Fynballa. "We grew in the same household, though we were not raised by our parents. All four of them died of a curious disease when we were very young."

"Who raised you then?" asked Amory, who had gradually caught up to them.

"An elderly couple of villagers," said Eoin. "They were gardeners and cooks by trade, since that was all they could physically do. They were the most generous and compassionate people we have ever known. They gave us the best of what they possessed, and they taught us how to live in an upright manner. The wife taught Fynballa to be a lady, and the husband raised me to be a man."

"What do you mean by upright?" Edna asked.

"All of Hertengard is meant to live according to a certain moral standard, called *Integritatem*. In a sense, it means that we must live selflessly and commit acts of consideration for others. Fyn and I were taught to do this to everyone we encounter, except in combative situations, and especially to each other. That is the reason I offered my shoes to Fyn."

"That is also why I declined the offer," added Fynballa, grinning.

"I wonder on whose standard *Integritatem* was founded," said Dilyn.

"Nobody knows," Fynballa said. "It was established after the beginning of the world. This is the standard by which our rulers cause the nations to either thrive or decay."

"What happened to those villagers who raised you?" Leona asked.

Both elves sighed deeply and glanced at each other with hesitation. Eoin finally answered, "When we were approximately twenty years old, only one decade by your standards, our village was raided by a squadron sent from the newly crowned Ever. The soldiers pilfered whatever looked or tasted appealing to them, including people, whom they would make slaves of the king. Everything else they destroyed by fire and blade and arrow. Our beloved guardians smuggled us into the nearby forest, where they bade us an eternal farewell and commanded me to provide for Fynballa from then on. As we ran from the smoke and chaos, we heard fatal screams from the couple who raised us. They returned to meet their doom."

Fynballa continued with a tear-struck face, "Ever since that day, we have been fugitives of the king, evading his troopers. We are young, able, and tradeless; therefore, he hunts us. We find temporary shelter and work wherever we can, but often there is little to be done with the fruitless land. Thankfully a kind farmer provided us two spare bedrooms last night during the tempest. Where were your chambers last night, or did you arrive at Hertengard today?"

"We had none," said Amory. "We arrived just before the storm hit and forced ourselves to go through it. I don't think that ended well. We were delayed."

"It is a wonder you weren't killed in a storm of that intensity!" exclaimed Eoin. "Even though we were never in the storm like you fortunate fools, we watched entire houses and silos collapse before finding shelter. We too were delayed, hence the soldiers finding us."

"Interesting," Dilyn muttered, "that we were both delayed by the storm, which forced our paths to cross."

Bernice looked up behind them and moaned. "What's more, it appears another storm's coming . . . and possibly this direction too. Are we close to Growan?"

"You can see it just beyond those firs," Eoin said. "We must hasten and find accommodations. Every home and lodge might be filled by now."

The Envoys, more than happy to finally be out of the vast forest, were quite pleased by the town they saw. Growan, set on an uneven plain, consisted of several buildings of wood and stone—mostly houses—which were all organized in the elvish fashion. The roads that divided the sections were many and complex, twisting and weaving in seemingly random ways, though with a bird's-eye view, they were a work of intricate art, forming what looked like a butterfly's wing. Every building that was not a house was either a market, smithery, cookery, butcher's shop, or logging station. Each workplace was surrounded by houses, evidently so the workers had no need to commute. The layout and amount of each workplace enclosed by homes worked together with all the others to form Growan's artistic overhead design.

The seven visitors entered the town jogging, hoping desperately to find a place to escape the squall. There were not many villagers outside at that point, but those who were seen were also hurrying to finish their business and head home. The Envoys discovered that both elves and dwarves resided here and were dressed similarly to how Fynballa and Eoin used to be. Eoin and Amory went into every lodging site, only to find each time that there was absolutely no vacancy. The seven ultimately found themselves on the complete other side of Growan, asking not only for directions to the next hotels (the villagers did not understand this term; their word for hotel is *lodge*) but also asking if the townspeople themselves would take them in.

Apparently seven was too many for anyone. At last, Eoin and Amory emerged from the last lodge, heads hung low.

"That is all," sighed Eoin as thunderclaps arose from the rapidly darkening sky. "There is no shelter available for us in Growan."

"Let's hope this storm's not as fierce as yesterday's," Leona said, "because we're going to brave the rain again."

"How could Nazir expect us to get anything done in this weather?" Amory asked aloud, despite the elven couple clearing their throats.

12

THE ROOK AND
THE QUEEN

The sun began to set on Hertengard again, making everything in sight appear more orange, just like the evening before. The Envoys, cloaked in their coats from Earth, and the two elves in their new attire began to shiver in the howling wind, trying to figure out how to escape the oncoming storm, or at least survive it.

"Are there any other towns nearby?" Amory shouted over the rapidly escalating winds.

"Nay," replied Eoin, "not for many a distance." (The humans did not know that a *distance* is an elven term of measurement and is equivalent to about half a human mile.) "Even if there were any, they would likely be as nonvacant as Growan is now."

"Are there any barns or something around here?" asked Leona.

"Any and all barns would likely be filled with people and beasts alike," said Eoin. "In addition, they would all be locked for the night."

"What else can we do?" exclaimed Fynballa. "The eastern forest from whence we just came is already at the storm's mercy, and there is nothing west, north, or south except for plains for several distances!"

"Pardon us," came two rugged, unknown voices.

The seven looked and saw a pair of young dwarves approaching them, one male and the other female. He had dirty blond hair and a short beard, and she had long red hair. They were both armored similarly to the Envoys.

The female spoke up again. "Sorry to interrupt, but are you searching for shelter from the storm, since you seem to be the only ones still outside?"

"Yes!" shouted everyone at once. "Where can we go?" asked Bernice.

"I'm Neisha, and this is my older brother, Nels. We're assistants at an orphanage a little further west. There's lodging for all of you, and the owner Ida would joyfully welcome you. Follow us!"

At that, the dwarves took off running, and the seven sprinted after them, not giving it a second thought. Within minutes, they were out of town and approaching a steep, rocky hill that rose about two hundred feet. Around the edges of the hill sat a continuous stone wall. The travelers ran around the hill to the lower, southern side of the it, where they saw the entrance, consisting of two large wooden doors inside a gap in the stone wall.

Dilyn looked back at Growan, which was still in sight, and saw that the storm now engulfed over half of the town and was swiftly advancing on them.

Nels and Neisha both pounded on the doors firmly, calling, "We're back with visitors! Let us in and hurry!"

Immediately one door was opened by an elf, and the sojourners began rushing in as the winds became mightier. The dwarfish siblings, holding onto protruding stones in the wall, remained at the door, making sure everyone else got safely inside the tall building into which the doors opened. Fynballa and Eoin were allowed to enter first, then Leona, Dilyn, and Edna.

At the instant Amory and Bernice were trudging through the door, a great gust blew against the entrance, sweeping to the left. Amory had managed to grab the door itself to avoid being blown away, but Bernice was holding onto nothing. She found herself being swept off her feet by the winds.

"Bernice!" Amory cried as he lunged back outside. The two dwarves had instantaneously grabbed her wrists, and with the help of Amory, pulled her inside, and the door was shut just before the rain hit.

"Are you all right?" gasped Amory.

"Yeah, I'm fine," Bernice said, grateful to be standing firmly again.

"What happened?" asked Edna, who was standing with the others a few yards from the doors. They were all unnerved when they saw Amory's eyes burning with anger.

"I am so sick of these storms!" he mumbled.

"You are one with everyone else in Liberdane," said Fynballa, "but thankfully we have shelter at last, and what quaint shelter it is, I might add!"

It was indeed a simple, yet charming building. It consisted of only one large room, and its walls were of almost-white stone and were decorated with many colorful, abstract, and often messy paintings, apparently created by artistic children. Short tables and cooking fires dotted the eerie space lit by torches on the walls and in the floor. Because of the rocky terrain, there were small amounts of stairs everywhere to connect the various levels of wooden flooring. Down the largest set of stairs at the back of the building came an elderly she-dwarf, who was also dressed and armed like the Envoys.

"Neisha! Nels! You made it back safely, and with guests! I'm so grateful and proud of you both!" she said with a wide smile.

"Thank you, Miss Ida," said Nels, turning to the visitors. "May I present the founder and director of *The Growan Haven for Children*, Ida. I'm sorry, I don't know all your names."

"I'm Eoin, and this is my betrothed, Fynballa. We are fugitives of sorts searching for accommodations and possibly work."

"I'm very pleased to meet you both," said Ida as she curtsied in greeting. "That's rather grand clothing for fugitives, I think."

"These so-called Envoys presented us with these garments earlier today when we met," said Fynballa.

Amory calmed down enough to introduce himself and his team. They all bowed after Ida curtsied again.

"Well, I can see you are more than just so-called Envoys of the Vine. You look legitimate to me!" Ida grinned. "I happen to be an Envoy myself if you couldn't tell, as are most of the staff and children here, including Nels and Neisha!"

"Wonderful," muttered Eoin.

"Well, it *is* good to meet you!" said Bernice.

"What brings a group of otherworldly Envoys into Liberdane?" Ida asked.

"Rather urgent, nation-sized business actually," said Amory, maintaining a perturbed, serious face. "Is there a place where we could discuss our plans with you and perhaps eat? The seven of us haven't eaten since noon."

"Of course! We'll head to the staff's quarters. Up this way."

Ida led the seven travelers, followed by Neisha and Nels, out the back of the entrance building into an open yard filled with odd wooden sculptures, which Fynballa said were playgrounds. They rushed through the torrential rain into the nearest building, which was even larger than the first. Neisha said this was where the children were housed and that the next cabin would be the staff's quarters.

Immediately upon entering, they heard the quiet sound of crying. Ida made a concerned expression as she continued to lead them through a long wooden hall with several doorways. The Envoys and elves glanced into the open doorways as they walked swiftly passed. What they saw in those rooms made them all stop short.

The elven and dwarfish children in those windowless rooms were crowded together, holding each other as tightly as possible. Some were crying, and all of them had immense fear in their eyes. There was only one adult per room, and none of them seemed able to console the children. Ida entered the room into which the visitors were staring.

"Is it the storms again, Twyla?" she asked a rather young elven girl (even younger than Fynballa) who appeared to be the adult in charge of the room.

"Yes," answered Twyla. "They are happening so frequently that the children think the world is ending! They will not let go of their fear."

Edna turned to Amory who was still looking frustrated. "I'm going to stay here awhile. Catch me up on your plans later."

Leona, Fynballa, and Eoin agreed to stay as well.

Amory sighed deeply. "All right. Do what you can to comfort these kids. They need it. They're lonely enough as it is. Just don't get too distracted from our real mission here." At that, Amory, Bernice, and Dilyn (who was now carrying both sets of elven armor) quickly followed Ida out of the children's chambers and into the staff's cabin.

Leona turned to Edna and the elves. "I'll take this room. The rest of you pick one and see what you can do. Encourage them, make them laugh, even cry with them if it helps. The goal is that they all eventually go to sleep."

The four dispersed, and they each entered a separate room according to their own gender. Fynballa hugged and consoled the lasses she was with and said constantly to remain strong. Edna described Earth to her group and told funny stories, which she and her parents experienced during their travels across America. Eoin sang melodies that he had composed himself; they were mostly about his many perilous adventures with Fyn. It was emotionally taxing work, but they all managed to calm the children to sleep within a couple of hours.

As Eoin checked all the doorways to ensure the children were asleep, he found the first room, where Leona was, still open. He peered through and saw Leona sitting at the foot of one of the wooden beds, where one last girl lay restless. Twyla stood nearby, her eyes filled with wonder.

"But I can still hear the storm!" said the small girl. "I cannot go to sleep if I know it is still here and could tear us apart!"

"Well, guess what?" asked Leona. "I don't believe this storm will tear us apart. I was actually in one last night with no shelter at all, just me and my friends!"

"How are you still alive?!" gasped the wide-eyed lass. Eoin wondered the same.

"Because Nazir was with us. Miss Ida, Miss Twyla, and all the others here have told you about him, and he's real! I knew he would protect us in the storm because he gave us a mission, and he was leading us. He didn't take the storm away, but he did protect us! He led us through the storm to meet two wonderful friends, who in turn led us to Growan, where we met Mister Nels and Miss Neisha, who then led us to you. Nazir helped us through the storm so he could lead us here to comfort you and tell you that he is here, watching over you!"

Eoin could see the girl's tense body relax, and she was soon asleep. Leona smiled and walked out of the room with Twyla closely following. Before Twyla closed the door to get some sleep herself, she said, "Thank you very much for everything! Your story about Nazir helping you means more than you know. None of the children—including myself—thought him to be that powerful, and we never even dreamed that he would perform such a miracle just so *we* could be comforted! This is proof that he does see and care for us orphans."

"I actually just made that connection as I said it," said Leona. "It's so crazy how Nazir works!"

"Indeed. Goodnight!"

Twyla shut the door, and Leona then discovered that Eoin had been watching. He wore a slight grin.

"You seriously believe in this omniscient Vine, don't you?"

Leona nodded and smiled. "Listen, we'd better find the staff's cabin and get some rest. I don't know how late it is, but I have a feeling tomorrow's going to be a hectic day."

"Edna and Fyn already left. There is no one else here and nothing else to be done. Let us be off."

They started off down the long hallway to the end of the building.

"Eoin, you said something I'm curious about. You told Ida that Fyn was your betrothed. I didn't know you were engaged; she wasn't wearing a ring."

"A ring? Why would she need a ring?"

Leona had to pause for a second. "Well, maybe it's done differently here, but on Earth, in most cultures—or at least in American culture—men give their betrothed engagement rings when they propose marriage to them."

Eoin gave her a swift, shocked glance. "That is absurd! If one did that here, then that would translate as buying a maiden's hand in marriage and bribing her!"

"For us it doesn't mean that at all. It means that the man thinks the woman as precious—or more precious—than the gold and gem in the ring. That ring is also the seal of the promise between them that they will marry each other. How did you propose to Fyn then?"

"I simply asked her if she would be my wife, and she graciously accepted. Our word was the only seal we ever possessed or needed, and after a decade, that covenant still stands! We would be wed by now if not for the king, who imprisoned the last remaining minister to abide by *Integritatem*. All other ministers are foul and wretched, demanding high compensation and even marrying of differing species! No, we will wait until that one good minister is freed or another arises."

"I hope you two marry soon, and I wish you both the best in that marriage!" said Leona.

"My thanks are yours."

Leona and Eoin arrived at the staff's chambers, which was very similar to the children's, and only Ida was there to greet them. She said that everyone else had gone to bed and that they would be given Amory's plans in the morning. She led them each to the rooms where the others were staying, and they bade goodnight and fell asleep on their prearranged mats almost instantly.

———

Leona awoke the next morning to Bernice shaking her. She opened her eyes and sat up drowsily, feeling all the soreness of yesterday's walking. Without windows, it was impossible to tell the time of day.

"What's the matter?" Leona asked.

"Time to go," Bernice said. "I'll tell you what's happening on the way out. Prepare for a battle."

Leona quickly got up, washed her face in a wooden bowl of water on a thin desk, and put on her armor. She followed Bernice, Edna, and Fynballa out of the room, where there was even more bustle. Some of the staff of elves and dwarves, about a dozen in all, hurried to put on their own Envoy armor. Among them was Amory, who kept everyone organized in a rather bossy way, and Dilyn, who made his way to his friends when he saw them.

"What's going on?" asked Edna.

"Amory wants to conquer and kill King Ever and Queen Gwenore and put new, better people in charge of Liberdane. He's decided to attack the tower where Queen Gwenore, Ever's ex-wife, lives," said Dilyn. "Ida says it's not far from Growan."

"How in the world did he come up with that decision?" Leona yelled.

Bernice sighed. "He was so mad at the storms and everything that's going wrong that he decided to overthrow the king and queen, who he said was the source of everyone's problems. When Ida asked him to consult Nazir on the matter, he said he was certain this was what Nazir wanted . . . that this was the object of our mission."

"Nazir said that we were supposed to reestablish his rule in Liberdane," said Edna. "Does that really mean killing off the current rulers?"

"Amory seems to think so," said Bernice.

"For what is everyone else preparing?" Fynballa chimed in, who was standing nearby with Eoin, looking very confused.

"They volunteered to help us with the invasion," Bernice said. "Ida herself had to stay with the children, but she begrudgingly asked if anyone wanted to go. These are the Envoys who said yes. Neisha and Nels will fight with us, as well as that elven girl, Twyla."

"How could they possibly be convinced to embark on such a feat?!" cried Eoin. "Some of these lads and lasses, especially Twyla, could not be older than thirty years of age, which is around eighteen by your standards! What of their duties here with the orphans?"

Bernice sighed deeper. "When Amory said that Nazir intended to reestablish his rule here and that overthrowing the king and queen seemed the only way for that to happen, Ida did not persuade him otherwise. She didn't want us to die in the process, so she recruited some of the staff to add to our numbers."

"Less than a score of soldiers—Nazir or no Nazir—cannot successfully take that rook!" said Fynballa. "The queen resides there, and it is therefore heavily guarded. You are the noblest and most compassionate people I have ever met, but your belief in this Vine will certainly be the death of you all."

Amory suddenly stepped in, looking a tad kinder than he was yesterday. "I would much rather die serving Nazir than sit idly by while innocent people suffer without knowing him. Are you two coming to help end the suffering? Your armor's next to Dilyn's bed."

"No, thank you," said Eoin sternly. "I would much rather die as an innocent fugitive than as a war criminal. I do wish you would stay, though. It would truly be wonderful to know you more and to hear your stories."

"Aye," Fynballa added, "but we will remain here and continue to care for the orphans, especially since there might be fewer workers after today. Perhaps we will even attain an occupation doing it. These children give me such joy!"

"You mean to get a job here?" asked Edna. "What if that brings Ever's troops here?"

"Then we will go on the run again, as usual, with any occupation we have ever held," said Eoin. "As such, I do not expect this job to be permanent, but as long as it lasts, we will be happy."

"Time to move," Amory called.

Leona and the others turned to their elven friends. She said, "Well, I want you to know there is a much better way to live, but all the same, I wish you both the best. Goodbye, and I hope we do meet again, so we *can* tell you our stories."

"Farewell," said Eoin, "and we hope for the same."

———

Everyone was finally ready. Amory led the squadron of Envoys down the hall, through the orphanage (which was uncharacteristically dry after the storm), and outside the wall at the foot of the hill. They bade a quick farewell to Ida, who shouted as they left, "May this mission be fruitful in preparing for the restoration of our land. For those of you who have worked here and even grown up here, fight for the children you've come to know so well, and hurry back!"

The warriors went around to the other side of the hill and went due north through a barren plain. Nels, who knew where the tower sat, and Amory led the way. Nels wore dark green armor and held a crossbow—one with wide, thin, and sharp limbs. His sister had turquoise armor and two hexagonal shields with a thick spike in each center. Twyla wore silver armor and was decked with an array of knives, some for throwing, others for wielding.

Before long, the Rook of Gwenore was in sight. It, like almost everything else in that world, was made of stone. It was round and dark gray and had no décor other than defense mechanisms, such as crossbows built into square windows and catapults set on the top. Dozens of massive goblin guards stood or sauntered around the fortress. A distance to its left was some fenced-in farmland riddled with scrawny cows making the most out of the blond grass. The Envoys hid behind a tall mound in the field and discussed their plans.

"How many guards would you say there were?" Amory asked the volunteers.

Bernice made a subtly appalled face, wondering why he didn't know this before.

"One or two hundred," said Neisha. "Half of them are posted outside and the other half in strategic places inside."

"How many entrances?"

"Two . . . the main gate and a back gate to bring in stores."

"Where is the queen usually?"

"On the fifteenth floor, the highest save the rooftop, where the most vigilant and accurate soldiers keep watch."

"All right," sighed Amory, "we obviously are too outnumbered to pull a frontal attack, so stealth will be key. We will enter the fortress through the back and make our way up to the queen. Nels, do you think the person who owns that farm will mind if we borrow his cattle for a distracting stampede at the front gate?"

"He probably would mind," said Nels sternly. "His livestock is weak enough as it is, and he lacks enough water and crops to reenergize them."

"Just tell him they're needed for Liberdane's redemption. Meet us in the tower when the cows are returned."

"He won't buy it, but all right," Nels called as he ran west toward the farm.

"I don't get this," said Dilyn. "If Gwenore is no longer the king's wife, then how does she still assume the title of queen, making this a good idea at all?"

"First, because no one took her place," replied Twyla. "Second, she performed a couple of political maneuvers to retain her power. She is separated from the king and therefore cannot rule Liberdane; however, she asserts her authority over this small sector of land. Really, all she rules is Growan, but she can be as ruthless as the king."

"Then today is the day her rule ends and Liberdane's freedom begins!" smiled Amory. "Forward, my friends, and let's reset Nazir's reign!" At that, Amory led the squadron to another mound closer to the tower and repeated the process until they were quite near the back gate. They had only waited a minute or two before they heard dozens upon dozens of thunderous hooves approaching. The Envoys glanced behind them and saw a line of perturbed cattle coming around to the front of the rook. Nels, riding a bull in the back of the line, roused the cows, using noises that might or might not have been intentional, since it was obvious he was barely staying on the bull. The alarmed guards hardly had time to respond to the assault. Some were trampled and others escaped and hid, but no one remained at his post.

The instant that all the cattle came to the front, the Envoys snuck through the unguarded back entrance. The first room they found themselves in was a large storage room, lit by the same kind of dim torches as those at the orphanage. Amory put his ear to the round-topped door at the end of the room. He heard voices and clanking and nodded to Dilyn. Dilyn, Twyla, and a couple of others who had long-range weapons stood ready about a yard from the door, while everyone else went behind where the door would swing. Dilyn put an arrow to the bowstring. Twyla swiftly unsheathed some throwing knives from her belt. Amory flung the door open, exposing the unsuspecting goblin soldiers to flying arrows and knives. As soon as every trooper within sight was dead, Amory led the charge out into a spacious room in the tower's center, where a spiraling staircase now crawling with guards stood, illuminated by a few frequent, round chandeliers dangling on a single chain that reached the bottom floor.

"Up the stairs!" Amory cried. "Give it your all and push through, whatever it takes!"

Amory led the charge, and the siege of Gwenore's tower began. Amory was bolting up the stairs, stabbing a soldier here, decapitating another there, hardly even slowing down. Bernice and Neisha were close behind him, watching goblins get impaled and bashed by their spear and shields. Edna was crumbling armor with her massive hammer, which soon made her fall back a tad. Leona had to get unnervingly close to the beasts in order to slay them with her axe, but because the monsters had such large weapons, it was not difficult to kill them when standing so close. Dilyn and Twyla brought up the rear, Twyla finishing whatever enemies were left alive from the charge, while Dilyn shot at troops ahead of the Envoys.

As Dilyn was gazing and firing upward, he saw flocks of arrows from enemy archers suddenly rain down on the attackers. The Envoys were forced to take cover in doorways along the stairway, whose end seemed further and further away. Twyla and Dilyn, now the only ones with long-range weapons still alive, shot back as much as possible, but by now there were over two dozen archers bombarding the intruders. Meanwhile, multiple soldiers with close-hand weapons began descending the stairs toward the pinned attackers.

"We can't stay at bay like this, or we're through!" called Amory. "Dilyn, think of something to shake them off fast!"

Just then, several larger arrows flew at the goblins from below. In a flash, the Envoys saw Nels with his crossbow leap onto a nearby chandelier, making it swing precariously toward the stairs. Avoiding enemy fire (mostly with the protection of his armor), he clung to the bottom of the chandelier with one hand, and with the other, sliced the chain holding the lower chandeliers with one swing of his sharp-limbed crossbow. The results were a deafening crash and the makings of a fire below, as well as a freer swing for the chandelier on which Nels clung. Nels climbed up the side of it and made it swing more and more until it was right above the stairs and the confused goblins, who were still getting closer to the other Envoys. At that point, Nels climbed to the top of the chandelier and cut that chain as well, right when it hovered over the stairs. Nels jumped off as the chandelier collapsed onto a guard and rolled down the staircase, sending many soldiers either fleeing or to their doom. Those who survived soon ran into the Envoys and died there. The path was clear for another moment.

"Upward!" cried Amory. "We can make it!"

They ran up and caught up to Nels, who was fighting off a couple more beasts.

"Thanks for coming so quickly," said Amory. "Nice weapon too!"

"You're welcome, and thank you!" said Nels between swings of his bow.

By then, everyone saw the smoke rising from the fire that was rapidly growing below. The Envoys knew that stone would not burn easily, but they would still need to hurry if they wanted to kill the queen and still escape the tower alive, and since the ground floor was almost completely in flames, their chances of survival were becoming slimmer and slimmer.

Eoin and Fynballa sauntered uphill toward the staff's chambers of Ida's orphanage, deep in thought. They had just finished playing with the children at their playgrounds but were not wholly focused. Not a word was spoken on their walk between there and the chambers. Eoin got to the door first and held it for Fynballa, who finally spoke up once inside.

"Interacting with the children was different without as many workers."

"Yes," said Eoin somberly. "They were much more joyful today, but I still sensed fear in their minds."

"It is likely due to the battle happening at the rook," Fyn said. "They are probably worried about the results of the battle if those Envoys fail."

Silence followed. Simultaneously the couple looked at each other, then slowly went back outside. They walked around the chamber building where the northern wall of the orphanage sat. The elves skillfully climbed it using protruding stone bricks. From the top, they could see the tower, its ground floor furiously ablaze. To the right of the tower, they were stunned to see a vast army gradually approaching the fortress. Eoin and Fynballa glanced at each other again, even paler than normal. Love, horror, concern, and confusion could be seen all at once in their eyes.

The Envoys were only a few floors away from the queen, whom they still had not seen. The smoke was getting thicker, and breathing was getting more difficult for everyone.

"Keep going!" coughed Amory, whose pace had become much slower. "Most of the soldiers are either dead or downstairs trying to put the fire out! We still have a chance!"

"And how about a chance for survival?" Leona spluttered. "Do you have any escape plans?"

Amory didn't have time to answer before they all came across a giant hobgoblin soldier in their way. He wore a green cape with his armor, and his helmet, which hid his face, had some tattered plumage. He unsheathed a five-foot-long broadsword.

"The captain of the guard!" shouted Neisha.

The captain spoke in a booming, thunderous voice to any troopers who could hear: "Open every window to let the smoke out! Everyone below me, see to that fire! Everyone with or above me, help snuff out these intruders! The leader in the blue armor is mine!"

Amory froze for a split second, then dodged the huge blade descending upon him. He scurried to a nearby room that was one of the guards' chambers. The captain angrily followed him inside, clearing the path for the other Envoys, which was what Amory intended. He had time to do nothing but dodge the giant sword as it smashed anything in its path. How he was going to kill this monster, Amory did not know, but he successfully kept it occupied while his team carried on.

Unless there was a goblin in front of her, Bernice kept her flag above every head to keep her comrades together. She and Leona took the lead, finding it difficult to pinpoint weak spots in the soldiers' armor. They eventually found that the necks, armpits, and thighs were the best places to hit, and each opponent would be defeated in a few strikes. For Edna and

Neisha, it didn't really matter where they hit as long as they continued doing it. Each blow they dealt, however out of breath they were, was devastating, and their opponents hesitated before charging at them, which always proved fatal. Dilyn and Nels stayed at the rear, aiming for soldiers who hadn't yet reached the front of their team, which numbered about twelve. They were right behind Twyla, who sometimes threw knives and other times went hand-to-hand with impressive finesse.

The Envoys were on the second to last floor when they ran into a tightly packed squadron of troops that reached the end of the staircase. The Envoys pressed on, causing a skirmish that helped no one gain any ground.

"We don't have time for this!" yelled one of the staff members, as everyone received scar after scar.

Without warning, everyone heard a couple of warriors' screams, and two elves, both armed with a sword and shield, emerged from one of the rooms with an open window, wreaking havoc on the goblins. One of them had red armor, and the other indigo, and they both had their hair bound in long ponytails coming from helmets, which had thin, decorative wings on either side. It didn't take long for the Envoys to realize that it was Eoin and Fynballa, and they zealously joined in taking out the last goblins.

"What made you change your minds?" asked Bernice as she stabbed a soldier in the neck.

"We care for you all," said Eoin as he beheaded another, "enough to want you to live! By our assistance in your mission, we hope to guide you to a way out, so that you will all live. A massive army is approaching us, so you will need to escape quickly. We used old fence posts to pole vault over the fire to the tower's outer wall, which we climbed up to get here. The room we entered after climbing had some rope which we can use to descend onto a nearby haystack, which was for the neighbor's livestock."

"How can we ever thank you?" asked Bernice.

"By ridding us of these wretched rulers and restoring our land, as you promised!"

It was at that point that the last goblins standing in the way of Queen Gwenore were dead. The Envoys hurried to enter her bedroom, which was filled with marvelous furniture and tapestries in purple and gold. The finest item was a king-sized bed with a curtained covering. Bernice had her head turned just in time for an arrow to fly from somewhere in the room and knock her helmet.

"That came from behind the bed!" Leona shouted.

Another arrow sped toward a giant, spiked shield decoration dangling over the doorway. The shield, now unattached to the wall, came crashing over the fragile entrance, causing the doorposts to collapse. Fynballa and Bernice were the only ones to jump through before the doorway became blocked; everyone else had to jump back out. More arrows came flying at the duo. Bernice threw her spear at the bed, making the firing cease long enough for Fynballa to charge, leap over the bed, and take a slash at the queen. Gwenore blocked it with a sword she had in one hand (the other held a crossbow).

The queen was about five and a half feet tall and had short, white hair. She wore a clear, golden crown with inlaid sapphire, though it seemed rather dull. Her dress and cape were crimson and gold. Her face was wrinkled well beyond her age, probably a result of violating *Integritatem*. Transformed though she was, her agility and skill with a sword had not diminished. She spun with almost every blow she dealt, and she dealt them rapidly.

Fynballa found herself using her shield far more than her blade. Gwenore ferociously pounded on her shield, though no damage seemed to be taken. As Bernice ran to retrieve her spear, the queen bent down, spun around, and swept Fyn's legs, knocking her to the ground. Gwenore had gotten on top of her when Bernice lunged at her from behind. Again, the queen managed to deflect it but, having to stand again, was now fighting both Bernice and Fyn. They heard a voice from outside the room saying, "Hang on! We've almost broken through the blockage. More guards are on us, though!"

The queen sneered at her opponents. "T'was a brilliant effort, but nonetheless foolish. You will all die in this tower, and for what? To kill someone who is not even in authority anymore? What a shame and a waste!"

Fynballa gritted her teeth. "This is for those decades of torment through which you put your own people!"

Fyn angrily started slamming her sword against Gwenore's, but the queen blocked every hit. Gwenore kicked Bernice out of the way, then did a jump kick that sent Fyn into the stone wall, her sword flying across the room and out of anyone's reach. She remained conscious but could not get back up. Gwenore then continued with Bernice. The queen tried to use the same kick but instead failed and received a hit to the stomach from the side of the spear. She quickly recovered and threw the same rapid, well-planned blows as before. Before long, Bernice could not keep up blocking. Gwenore used both her sword and crossbow to spin the spear in Bernice's hands far enough to make her drop the spear in pain. The queen kicked the spear aside, near a hyperventilating Fyn, and put Bernice against another stone wall, their faces inches apart.

"You have the skill of an amateur," whispered Gwenore mockingly. "That imaginary Vine of yours should have trained you longer before 'sending' you here! I've killed many Envoys with far more experience."

A tumbling sound from the doorway followed. Edna had managed to make a hole in the rubble with her hammer, and now Dilyn was raining arrows toward Gwenore. She ducked, and Bernice evaded the onslaught. Without warning, Fynballa got up, grabbed Bernice's spear, and leapt onto the distracted queen, impaling her through the heart.

For a moment, everyone was still, letting it sink into their minds that their attack was a success. Eoin spoke up first.

"We must make haste if we're to escape alive. The base of the tower is beginning to collapse. Let us make a hole in this blockage large enough for Fyn and Bernice to crawl through, then we will make for our window."

Bernice shouted through the hole, "And don't forget Amory! Where is he?"

Amory was doing a tad better at keeping up with the goblin captain. He dodged his giant sword and succeeded in striking him once or twice. He was uncomfortable with blocking the captain's huge swings, not because he doubted his *sword's* strength but because he wasn't sure of his own. After demolishing the guards' chambers, the captain forced Amory back onto and down the stairway. Amory ducked, dodged, and shot in whenever he got the chance. He nonfatally slashed the beast a couple more times, but the captain just seethed through the pain and kept swinging.

Gradually the whole tower began to sway. The integrity of its foundation and first floor was all but gone. Amory and the monster fought for balance, doing their very best not to fall off the stairway and into the fire. Amory knew he had no time. No one seemed to be beating the other, and he had to kill this last foe now while there might be a slim chance of escape.

I hope the others got to the queen by now, he thought.

"Face it, child," roared the captain. "No one in this tower is coming out alive. It does not matter which of us kills the other. You and I have both lost!"

The beast started wielding again, and Amory frantically ran into him, trying in vain to push him over the stairway's edge.

"Nazir, make a way out!" he called.

Instantly he felt the captain rear back and heard him yell in pain. The monster leaned back and fell off the edge, a small arrow in his hidden face.

Amory heard a voice behind him. "Well, I'm not Nazir, but maybe I can help!"

In all the smoke and swaying, it was hard for Amory to determine who it was at first. He then saw it was a man with a cutlass, a golden shield, black and red armor, and a miniature crossbow on his wrist.

13
ALLIANCE AND DIVISION

The tower started to sway even more, and Amory struggled to remain standing as he gasped, "Ambrose! What the heck are you doing here?"

"I'll explain after we get out," Ambrose coughed as he trudged toward Amory. "Is anyone else from your crew here?"

Amory didn't need to answer, for the rest of the Envoys—including Eoin and Fyn, to Amory's shock—were just descending the staircase. The humans, especially Dilyn, were just as surprised as Amory.

Ambrose continued, "Now before you guys ask too many questions as to how I got here, I came to kill the queen and give you a way of escape."

"The queen's already dead," Bernice called out.

"I assumed as much. Now follow me! I have friends with wings waiting outside these windows for us. Pick a room, and they should fly us out before this tower falls!"

Everyone dispersed to the four nearby rooms. Waiting at each window were large, winged creatures, such as griffins and rocs. Twyla, Neisha, Edna, and Fyn (at Eoin's insistence) got out first. Next were the rest of the orphanage workers, including Nels, for a couple of rounds. During their flights, the tower began leaning to one side (for those still in the tower, it leaned forward). After the workers went Dilyn, Leona, Bernice, and Eoin. By then, the rook bent almost thirty-five degrees. It finally started to freefall by the time two rocs returned for Amory and Ambrose. This time, the rocs didn't alight at the windows, they simply caught each man after they had jumped out. They flew out from under the tipping tower as it plummeted to the ground in a heap of stone and smoke. The pair of rocs landed where they had dropped off the others, amidst a large group of diverse, armed creatures.

Ambrose called to his army, "A hundred of you, put out the rest of the fire before it incinerates this whole, dry field! If you can't find water, use your other materials."

"I believe thanks are in order," Amory said not only to Ambrose but to Eoin and Fynballa. "Now, how did you get here, and who are all these soldiers?"

"We are the Self-Worthy," said Ambrose proudly. "A group seeking to reveal to everyone their individuality. We've come here to end King Ever's reign and establish one of peace and fulfillment for all!"

"You didn't happen to pass by Nazir on your way through worlds, did you?" asked Bernice.

"I didn't have to," said Ambrose, unsheathing the Sword of *Chârâsh* from a belt on his chest, hidden in his red cloak. It instantly glowed a bright green.

Leona recognized it. "That's the Sword from Azarias's forge! He said it was super special."

"Ah, so you know of this blade," said Ives, emerging from the throng. "It is remarkable that he managed to get it."

"Yeah," Leona mumbled.

"This is the group you joined?" asked Dilyn. "What did they do to persuade you that Nazir didn't do?"

Ambrose smiled fondly at his younger brother. "Man, I missed you, Dilyn! I was wanting to talk with you, to do some catching up, and to tell you about this cause. I thought you might like it. To answer your question, they appealed to me and my desires. Nazir seems only interested in his own agenda, while the Self-Worthy's is my own. We want to contribute to everyone realizing their own selves and potential and help them become the absolute best that they can be."

"How could you say that Nazir's only interested in himself? He died for you!" exclaimed Leona. "He knows you can't realize your own potential without him because we're broken beyond mortal repair! He's the only one who can fix you!"

Ives was about to retort, but Ambrose cut in. "I never said I was against him. I thought perhaps I could try to follow both him and Maewing, our leader."

"That is preposterous!" said Ives. "Maewing would never allow it!"

"Everyone knows you can't serve two masters," Amory added.

"Why not?" Ambrose smirked. "Amory, let me tell you something. All these creatures and I were on our way to attack Diamond Culet and overthrow King Ever. Then we saw the queen's tower on fire and goblins outside going crazy. Maewing had said it would be a good idea to see to Gwenore as well as Ever, so we decided to help whoever had attacked. I never expected the invaders to be Envoys, but that got me excited all the more.

"Face it, Amory. The Envoys and the Self-Worthy are virtually the same. We both strive and fight for peace and fulfillment, and we mean the best for the common individual. You guys would've been dead by now if not for us. You wouldn't have escaped without my intervention, and even if you had, how do you think all these troops outside died? Certainly not by the stampede your young dwarf friend caused; it was over as fast as it had begun. Guys, we've all got the same goal in mind: Ever's death and resulting prosperity in Liberdane. If you're going to accomplish your mission, Amory, you need us. You can't take Ever without serious numbers."

"And what's in it for you?" asked Amory. "Do you need us?"

"No, but I want you," Ambrose said, then turned to Ives. "I don't agree with everything Maewing says and does, and as an individual, I'm entitled to my own opinion. The Envoys, I believe, fill in the gaps." He turned again to his human friends. "What do you say? Will we join forces and indefinitely free Liberdane?"

Amory looked at his comrades. "Is there anyone opposed of joining them?"

Only Edna and Neisha raised their hands.

"This mission was given from Nazir to us Envoys alone," Edna said sternly. "I don't feel good about linking arms with a group that doesn't believe in him."

"We're going to attack the castle anyway, whether or not you're with us," said Ambrose. "It's just a matter of if we must kill a few more enemies to ensure a securely peaceful rule."

"Oh, so you're threatening us to join you," Edna replied.

"We must make haste, one way or another," said Ives. "It is a few days' journey to Diamond Culet, and there are likely already goblin messengers on their way to warn the king."

Eoin stepped in, looking uncommonly bold. "As for me, I simply want the king dead; I care not by whose hand he dies. It is only sensible to fight with the larger forces. Whether or not you Envoys join, Fyn and I are."

That was the decision maker for Amory. Not wanting to lose the elves to whom he knew Nazir had led them, he extended his hand. "All right, Ambrose. We're in." The following handshake was one Amory would long remember.

The Self-Worthy armies, now intermixed with Envoys, began to march again to the northeast, where Ives said Ever's fortress lay. Most of the orphanage workers decided to return to Ida and the kids, but Twyla, Nels, and Neisha wanted to stay with these new Envoys, feeling that Nazir wanted them to. Amory thoroughly thanked them all.

It was soon decided that the Self-Worthy, because of their numbers, would initiate a frontal attack on Diamond Culet while the Envoys, who were obviously skilled with stealth, would sneak inside, open the front gates for the Self-Worthy if necessary, and tear the castle apart from the inside. Everyone agreed with this plan.

After the first night, which was spent in innovative, portable tents, they all arose early and set off again. During that morning, Dilyn found his way to Ambrose, who led the multitude.

"So how are you liking this group of yours?" Dilyn asked.

"Dilyn, I've never felt more fulfilled! Here, I matter and I'm seen! All my life, I've wanted to influence people for the better, to contribute to the good in their lives. Now I am, and I never thought I'd start so early!"

"Well, I'm happy for you."

"What about you, bro? Do you feel like you're making an impact with the Envoys?"

Dilyn sighed and thought for a second. "I don't know, honestly. I know I did the right thing by accepting and believing in Nazir . . . something I really wish you'd consider doing . . . and I know he changed me. That said, I thought I'd be making a real difference by reestablishing Nazir's reign here. I mean, I helped kill the queen and everything, but I'm only alive to say that because of you and your group—thanks, by the way."

"What can I say?" said Ambrose. "We have power in numbers, and you're welcome."

"That's the thing. I feel a lot safer and more comfortable with you guys than with my friends back there. I have a feeling that that shouldn't be a deciding factor, but I don't know. I feel like I'd be more seen and impactful with you."

"I know you would be if you joined us! You'll never regret it!"

Dilyn wasn't so sure.

Another couple of days went by, and it seemed as though they had gotten no closer to Ever. The dying trees and blond plains never ended. At one point, the Envoys (except for Dilyn, who mostly stuck with his brother now), plus the elven couple, were altogether as they trekked along, growing quite tired of strolling and marching. It was then that Fynballa, who had been oddly quiet the past few days, decided to speak her mind.

"I do not feel well about all this anymore."

"About what?" asked Bernice.

"Overthrowing the king. I no longer believe that it is just."

"How could you say that?" asked Eoin with wide eyes. "They deserve death for all that they have done!"

"Fyn, you're the one who killed the queen," said Amory. "Don't you feel a sense of accomplishment and satisfaction from that?"

"I feel quite the opposite, actually. I feel like less of the woman I was a week ago. I feel emptier."

"But she violated *Integritatem*!" Eoin said.

"Who is to say I did not by killing her? I could very well be a murderer!"

"Fyn, do not even say that!" gasped Eoin. "I know you, and you are no such thing!"

"But Gwenore was our queen! She had a right to enforce laws, no matter how unjust they were. I had no right to oppose her."

"She was not the queen when we fell upon her, not rightfully. By right of law, I believe you did have the right to contradict her."

"Which law says so, Eoin? My love, what has come over you? You, who initially thought it wrong to oppose authority, have become obsessed with assassination, and it has turned you into something of a beast!"

"And your sudden pacifism has turned you to a spineless coward! These Envoys presented us with armor and weapons! What do you think was the purpose of that?"

"What did Nazir say it was for again, Amory?" asked Edna.

"I think it was to conquer the king and queen, but I actually don't remember," Amory said.

"I want our current rulers gone because I love you, Fyn, and I want to protect you from any more dangers they cause. I am sick of evading goblins, and when I finally began to fight back in a way that hurt them more severely, I knew this could end everything that troubled us in the past. Do you not desire an end to our suffering, to our state as fugitives?"

"I saw how fiercely you fought in the tower," said Fyn, "and that makes me very proud of you, but what makes me love you the most is the fact that you stand for justice, at least until now."

"I still am, do you not see? Are you that blinded by the death you witnessed and caused that day? I thought you were a warrior, Fyn. I thought you were stronger than that."

Fynballa stopped short, which made Eoin and the Envoys stop as well. The Self-Worthy were still marching forward when Fyn started walking the other way.

"I need not be a part of this," she said. "This is wrong, and I am only sorry I did not see it sooner. I am withdrawing, and I do not need you to come with me, Eoin. You go kill the king. Pursue your pleasures, just as he does! But I cannot be with you if you do."

Eoin did not follow her. "I do not need you to be with me! I can find someone else who is not squeamish about killing those who must face justice!"

Fynballa stopped, took off her armor piece by piece, and tossed them in his direction, tears rolling down her face. "Then these are for her!"

At that, she ran off in the same attire and fearful temperament as when the Envoys first found her.

Eoin bundled up her armor, slung it over his shoulder, and walked on with the rest of the Self-Worthy. The appalled and panicked Envoys quickly followed him. Leona sprinted up and stood in front of him.

"Eoin, what are you thinking?! She's your fiancée! Are you going to just desert her after all these decades?"

"My business is with the king now. My eyes are fixed on his ruin. If she does not support me in this quest, then she is no longer my betrothed."

"But you both promised each other that you'd marry! Listen to yourself, Eoin. Are you going to give up all the joy of being with her just to kill someone?"

"That is but a small price for our nation's liberation, and if I recall correctly, she forsook her promise first by turning around."

Leona could think of nothing else to say, nor could anyone else. She looked at Amory, who was pale with fear and guilt that the mistake might be his own.

An hour or so later, the armies stopped for lunch, which was only cheeses and produce from other worlds. They had no time to cook any meat; they needed to reach Ever's fortress as soon as possible while they still had the element of surprise.

The dark, looming castle was within view now, amidst the hazy horizon. It brought chills through everyone's spines, though they knew it should have made them feel happy. The troops sat in small groups as they ate, the seven Envoys being in one. They all either looked down despondently or stared at Eoin, who for the first time in decades ate alone.

"You know," said Nels, with his mouth full of cheese, "I'm starting to feel as Fynballa does about all this."

"You too?" sighed Amory.

"Gwenore's tower is a pile of ashes and rubble now, and it's because of me. I feel guilty, and that's a sign that I did something Nazir doesn't approve of."

"I think we all feel that way," said Twyla.

"As do I," said Eoin, sauntering in their direction. "I am alone for the first time in I know not how long, even though I am in the company of thousands. In that loneliness, I began to ease my temper and consider what I just said and did. I must confess that Fynballa was correct. Ever and Gwenore are our authorities, and they deserve respect because of that alone. Amory, what if you did something your group disliked or disagreed with? Would it not be dishonoring for them to forcefully replace you or even simply shout in your face about everything you did wrong?"

"I did make some mistakes lately regarding this mission," Amory said, "and they did no such thing. They followed me even though they knew it was wrong."

"And I don't think we should have," said Bernice. "We should've done what Fyn did and left when the line was crossed. Actually, we should've come to you and discussed our issue with you first and then left if no change was made."

"You leaving would've made me come to my senses sooner," said Amory.

"Just as Fyn's departure opened my eyes," Eoin continued. "What the king and queen do is for a reason, good or ill, and it is wrong for us to rebel against them. We can only hope they have a change of heart—or at least the king, now—and perhaps we can contribute to that. For these reasons, I must find Fyn and makes amends with her, so I too will be withdrawing."

Eoin began strolling back the way he had come, carrying a sack with Fynballa's armor and wearing his own, as Amory and the others quickly stood up.

"Wait for us," Amory called. "We'll join you!" Just then, they saw Ambrose, Dilyn, Ives, and Esorbma walking past them.

"Maewing would never allow this," Ives muttered into Ambrose's ear. "To link up with true Envoys is calamity waiting to strike!"

"What's her excuse with Lisias?" Ambrose whispered back in a volume unintentionally heard by the Envoys.

"He only joined us after he rejected the Vine."

"We can be inclusive, can't we?"

"Wait, you have people who rejected Nazir in your ranks?" asked Amory. The brothers, elf, and doppelgänger stopped immediately.

Esorbma chuckled as he turned to the Envoys. "Well, I wouldn't say they rejected him, so to say. They just decided to try something new."

"Besides that, Lisias is a good friend of mine," said Ambrose. "It's not like he's the opposite of an Envoy. He still has many of Nazir's good traits, like honor and leadership."

"He forsook the love and plan Nazir freely gave him?" asked Amory.

"Well, Nazir says, 'Once an Envoy, always an Envoy,'" Edna put in. "Just because he doesn't follow the Vine anymore doesn't mean he's not his child now. That never changes."

Amory stared at Ambrose. "Even so, it was a mistake to join you guys. We will not go and kill the king. We're leaving." At that, the seven of them turned to leave.

Ives called out, "We are still going to battle, and if we find you anywhere near that castle, we cannot guarantee that you will be spared."

The Envoys kept walking until Leona turned around and said, "Dilyn, are you coming or what?"

Dilyn hesitated a long while and looked back and forth between his friends and his brother. Finally, he decided, "I think I'll stay here. I don't intend on killing the king either, but I do want to . . . keep an eye on these guys here, if that's OK."

Amory, who was with Leona, said, "That is your choice, Dilyn—not mine and not your brother's. But you just heard about someone in this group who left Nazir. If you do this, that's what you're doing. I'm telling you right now that you won't find what you think you will in that group. Only Nazir can complete you."

"I'm not leaving you," said Dilyn. "I still have my Dagger, and I fully intend on continuing to talk with Nazir, the same as before. I just want to see what these guys are like."

The Self-Worthy horn blew, a signal to the troops that it was time to move out again.

"Forward, my friends!" called Ives. "Tonight, we fall upon the king and finally free this land!"

There grew a great commotion of creatures going this way and that, trying to get back into line. Dilyn and Ambrose were swept into the fray and out of sight.

"Dilyn!" Amory and Leona called. "Dilyn! Come back! This is wrong. This is not what Nazir called us to do!" they shouted in vain. They looked at each other with great worry.

"I'm sorry," Amory said. "All this mess is because of my brashness."

"You're forgiven," Leona said hastily. "Let's find Eoin."

They caught up with the rest of the group. The elf was not with them.

"Where's Eoin?" Amory asked.

"We haven't seen him yet," said Nels, "but let's see if we can pick up the pace and catch up."

The seven began to jog due south. All they carried were their weapons; they had left all else behind. They did not stop to rest, hide, eat, or drink.

After about half an hour, their jogging turned to running. They bolted through a long, thin plain with short hills on either side. They shouted both elves' names, but their voices just bounced back to them. Finally, they had to stop (the dwarves were having trouble keeping up).

"Where in the world could they have gone?" gasped Bernice.

"Perhaps we ran in the wrong direction," suggested Twyla.

Instantly from behind the hills on both sides, hobgoblins sprang forth, roaring and flailing their weapons. The Envoys positioned themselves to fight but quickly saw that they were surrounded by dozens of troops, blades pointed and crossbows readied.

The largest soldier stepped forward and threw down an open cloth wrap. "Put down your weapons, now!" he screamed.

With hesitance, Amory dropped his sword, and everyone eventually followed suit, though Leona and Nels objected.

"We can't give up our search!" Leona said.

"Search for what? For whom?" a second goblin creaked. "If you happen to mean the she-elf who killed the queen, then tell us now! His highness has put a price on her head, and if you tell us where she is, we will consider turning you loose."

"I tell you the truth, we do not know where she is, though we have heard of her," Amory said.

"But is she the one for whom you were searching?" asked another goblin.

"No," Amory replied in vague honesty.

"Off with you armor too," said the first trooper. "We know you wear some like hers, and we know you know each other. That is the reason for which you are all under arrest by his majesty's direct command, for assistance of assassination, military assault, and destruction of the king's property."

The Envoys took their armor off, and the goblins put them with the weapons in the wrap. One soldier took one more glance at Amory, peered at his belt, and pointed at it.

"That dagger comes off too! And if you all have daggers or other hidden weapons, take them off in two seconds before we rip them off you, slicing you if necessary!"

The prisoners begrudgingly complied and were soon bound and forced to walk with the goblins on the other side of the western hills, where an underground trapdoor lay open and guarded by a couple more troops.

"Where are we going?" Bernice asked shakily as they trekked down the stairs below the trapdoor.

"This passageway leads directly to Diamond Culet. There, you will be interrogated by the king himself, then imprisoned and enslaved for however long he desires."

Bernice looked ahead at Amory, who was looking back at her. She thought he never looked so scared.

14
VENGEANCE IS TAKEN

Musty, underground smells filled the tight air as the Envoy prisoners were jostled through the passageway by the gleeful hobgoblins. A torch hung every several yards, so most of the time they groped forward in the dark, pushed by the captors to keep moving at a physically taxing pace. Just when the captives felt like they couldn't go any further, they saw another trapdoor open ahead of them—a dim, fiery light peeking through.

The soldiers and Envoys climbed out of the passageway and into Diamond Culet, engulfed in an orange dusk. The sights that met the new prisoners filled them with horror. Fire, metal, stone, and suffering were everywhere. The Envoys couldn't look anywhere without seeing elven and dwarfish slaves cutting stone, fortifying the ominous stone walls, crafting wooden scaffolding, forging weapons, digging dry trenches, boiling meat or vegetables, or getting beaten by vicious soldiers.

The castle itself consisted of five massive towers, each reaching six stories in height. Between each tower were thick, two-story walls with rooms throughout, each measuring about a third of a mile long. A large, open courtyard lay in the center of the castle. At the southernmost tower (which could be considered the front) was the gate and the portcullis. At the northeastern tower, on the very top floor, was the throne room, where the Envoys were taken. This room seemed to be moved into recently, for it was riddled with open crates, rich furnishings, and pleasant-looking beverages and food. In addition, the throne was crooked. On that throne, sitting rather sloppily, was King Ever himself.

The elven king was even paler and more wrinkled than his former queen, which made him look like the most frightening and intimidating creature in all Hertengard. However, he did manage to keep his white hair (or what was left of it) groomed and trimmed, and he wore lush, crimson garments with a golden cape and a bejeweled sword. His winged crown, which appeared transparent, had fluid gold melded into it and was also adorned with otherworldly rubies. However, it bore several black smudges.

Upon seeing the Envoys, the king instantly sat up, teeming with interest. "Speak and identify yourselves!" he shouted in his shrill, creaky voice.

The prisoners were put in front of the throne. The backs of their knees were stricken, so they were forced to kneel. Amory added his own bow as he said, "We are all Envoys of the Great Vine Nazir, King of *Rôb Tëbél*."

"Ah," said Ever, "so you *are* the ones whom my messengers reported to have assassinated my queen, or at least helped to assassinate. I will inform you now that I intend to keep you enslaved for a very long time for this, but your captivity could be temporary if you truthfully answer this one question: *Where is your accomplice, the she-elf who actually did the evil deed?*"

Amory looked the king in the eye, despite every fear that crept into his head. "I truthfully answer you in saying none of us know where she is. We were searching for her fiancé, who in turn was searching for her, but we did not find either."

The king sat back a tad. "How did you get separated?"

"We had a heated debate on whether or not to come here and kill you. That she-elf, feeling the guilt of killing the queen, was the first to relent in the pursuit. Eventually we all did, but some of us—myself included—were slower to realize our wrongful actions. We acknowledge and accept that you, O Ever, King of Hertengard, are the authority here and should not be challenged by your own people."

Ever sat still for a few slow moments, a grin gradually creeping across his face. "I am pleased to see some respect for once. I have not experienced such in years, except from my own men. But of course a representative would appeal to me, which means you likely want something from me. Now, out with it! What do you desire?"

"But, your majesty, we want nothing from you," said Amory before he had an idea, ". . . except that you lend your ear to a small proposal."

"What is it?" asked the king impatiently.

"That you come with us to meet someone . . . Nazir, the King of the multiverse himself. I know he'd be delighted to see you!"

"Is that all?" Ever chuckled. "I have been given that same proposal frequently throughout my fifty-year reign, and even before that! Each time, I declined because I see no use or proof of the existence of this Vine. It fails to coincide with the standards of life."

"Do you mean *Integritatem* or your own standards?" Amory asked.

"Silence!" the king shrieked. "Just as I suspected; as soon as I decline your offer, your respect for me fades! Well, you will be made slaves nonetheless. Take them away!"

Before anyone could say another word, the Envoys were jerked away from the king's presence. They were taken down to the courtyard again and to the western corner. There, they were forced down another trapdoor (this one being far larger and more secure) to what appeared to be the dungeon, which was a long, simple aisle with a row of cells on either side. The endless cells seemed to house only slaves, all of whom either sat or lay stone-faced, simply waiting for their next grueling task.

After several minutes of marching, the troops and captives stopped, and the Envoys were each put in one of seven cells in a row on the left side. The slam of the shutting pen doors echoed through the whole dungeon.

"See you tomorrow, bright and early!" snickered one of the guards.

As more slaves were marched into the prison for the night, Amory looked at his cell: a simple, unlit room with nothing on the ground or the walls but dirt. He sat in a corner as expressionless as the slaves who'd been there for years.

"Thanks a bunch, Amory," said Edna. "Why'd you have to say that last part to Ever? Now, we might never get out!"

"Don't let those thoughts into your head so early," said Twyla calmly enough. "There is still hope for escape!"

"Quiet!" said another guard. "There is no escape, especially for you! No more noise, and get some sleep before I send you to work the night shift!"

As the guard walked away, Neisha mumbled to her brother, "We should never have come."

"Let's face it: we deserve to be in here," said Bernice. "We actually committed a crime, and we're being held responsible for that."

"But no crime is worth this much suffering, right?" Twyla interjected.

"Actually every crime deserves worse," Leona sighed. "Boy, my mom's probably going to wonder where I am after I don't return."

"Quiet!" the guard bellowed again.

Amory just sat there, completely silent, feeling more alone, afraid, and distrusted than he was as an abandoned boy.

Nazir, I'm so sorry! I twisted your words according to my own plans and desires, and now I'm reaping the consequences. I drove myself to do things I would never want done to myself, and I got distracted from my main mission of representing you in this dark world. The two elves you gave to us are long gone, and all we've taught them is that you overthrow evil rulers. While King Ever will be held accountable for all he's done, you're still letting him reign, but why? He's the one in the way of people seeing you, the one who's keeping your kingdom from being reestablished! I guess you have your reasons, but I don't understand. With all that aside, I'm now being held accountable for what I've done, and if I could set things right, I would in a heartbeat. Even so, please be with me, Nazir! Please see me and strengthen me—all of us—in this moment. Please be with us, Father!

Because of all the walking that day, it wasn't long until Amory fell asleep, repeating the words, *I failed you, Father. Be with us, Father. . . .*

———

Slam! Slam! Slam! Crash!

Amory was startled awake by several constant thumps coming from the front gate. He heard faint shouts and war cries, as well as arrows whizzing and a few blades clashing. Amory quickly got up and heard others do the same.

"The Self-Worthy," he heard Bernice mumble, "they got through!"

As Amory watched the prison guards sprint toward the dungeon entrance, he became even more anxious. *If the Self-Worthy find us here, they'll kill us, just as they'd threatened!* he thought.

Everyone suddenly felt the whole castle rumble as they heard the giant portcullis collapse; the Self-Worthy had breached the mighty fortress. The running, stamping, flapping, and fighting sounded much more intense, and multiple creatures were heard shouting, "Freedom! Freedom for Liberdane!"

For a few short minutes, nothing beyond the fighting was heard. Then, the captives heard the dungeon trapdoor being yanked open. The hobgoblin guards were trampled easily enough by three Self-Worthy minotaurs who came through (a fourth one died in the scuffle). One of them grabbed the key from one of the dead guards.

"Secure the entrance. I'll start at the back and work my way to you," one of them said. "Fear not, former slaves! We've come to free you! You are captives no more!"

Amory didn't recognize the minotaur as it jogged his direction. His heart stopped when it glanced at him and did recognize him. The minotaur stopped midstride and turned to him, then paced backwards slowly, seeing all the other Envoys in their cells.

"Well, well, well," it chuckled. "So you made it here after all, just as Ives predicted! Then he won't be surprised when I show him your corpses!"

It bolted to Amory's cell door, fiddling with the key in one hand and holding a menacing scimitar in the other. Amory scrambled to the back wall as the beast, snickering, put the key in the hole. It instantly stopped and looked to the entrance, where it heard two deathly yowls from its comrades. Right in front of Amory's cell, the minotaur was swiftly overtaken by two slender, armored elves.

"Eoin! Fyn!" Edna gasped. "How in the world did you get here?"

"The tale shall be told in a moment," said Eoin as he took the stolen key. He then freed the Envoys, telling the story as he did so. "I found Fyn going to a nearby village. I told her that I was wrong to pursue the king and deeply apologized for my behavior, and she undeservedly forgave me. After I returned her armor to her, we went searching for you, since you said you would come with me."

"We were a tad delayed," Leona said.

"We concluded that. We came over the eastern slopes of that small valley when we beheld the seven of you surrounded by goblin soldiers. We took cover, knowing they were searching for us as well, and silently followed them to the secret passage. We knew then that you would be taken to Diamond Culet, so we sprinted there. We already knew that the Self-Worthy would besiege the castle that night, but we knew not what they would do to you. Keeping out of sight, we arrived near the Culet and waited for the attackers to come and begin their assault. When they did, we snuck through the fray and found you!"

The Envoys were now free. Amory bowed low. "I can't thank you two enough, but truthfully we don't deserve to be freed."

"Nonsense!" said Fynballa. "You have yet to free us from oppression, and that is your mission, is it not?"

"Hey!" called one of the nearby slaves. "Are you going to simply leave us here?"

"Nay, friend!" Fyn replied. "We shall take this opportunity to rescue you all! We will not free our friends without freeing you as well, you who have suffered for so long. What say you, Amory?"

Amory grinned, "Let's get started."

Eoin smiled as he sprinted to the back of the dungeon, beginning to unlock every cage. More rumbles and shouts were heard overhead. Fynballa and Nels briefly went back outside to retrieve the Envoys' equipment, knowing they were stored nearby. They returned unnoticed by their enemies, and the Envoys quickly rearmed themselves.

"Now," Amory said as he buckled his belt and sheath, "our best course of action is to take the slaves through the secret passage, out of the battle. The nine of us will form a protective line between the prison and the passageway's entrance, keeping the Self-Worthy and the goblins at bay. Beyond that, avoid battle with Ever and his men at all costs; our only objective is to get the slaves out of here. Understood? Once the last prisoner gets through, we'll shut the entrance and go with them. Hopefully, we can help them establish a livelihood again and tell them about Nazir."

"There must always be an angle with Nazir, must there?" sighed Fynballa.

Finally, the last cage was opened and the last captive released.

"We are ready!" Eoin shouted.

"All right, then," said Amory. "For Liberdane, and for Nazir!"

At that, he led nine of them bursting through the dungeon entrance, being careful not to make any unnecessary noise. They quickly formed the protective barrier, and Amory, at the front of the line, opened the secret trapdoor. He then beckoned the slaves to hurry inside and to keep running until they got to the end of the tunnel.

Beyond the Envoys and slaves, the battle raged everywhere under the veil of night. Every tower, wall, and inch of the central courtyard was filled with goblins and Self-Worthy troops. Several sections of wall and scaffolding were in flames, and the main entrance—excluding the tower—was in rubble. The portcullis, fallen and bent, lay amidst piles of debris and bodies of both defenders and attackers. On top of the entrance tower, Leona caught a glimpse of Dilyn among other archers, raining arrows over the desperate goblins.

The Envoys had been stealthy enough that it took a few minutes for the goblins to spot them. Once they were in sight, though, the Envoys soon got quite busy fending off soldiers. Amory, Leona, Bernice, Neisha, and the elven couple found themselves fighting off multiple opponents at once, but Edna, Twyla, and Nels, having large or long-range weapons, were able to help the others out frequently. When Dilyn saw his friends, he also subtly shot down any goblins around them (but any of the Self-Worthy who attacked them, he would not touch). Dilyn looked for Ambrose and found him going with Ives and Esorbma to the tower with the throne room.

———

From the throne room window, King Ever watched with great anxiety. Flanked by his two largest guards, he fired arrows from his crossbow on anyone who didn't look like a goblin, whether it was one of his own men or not. Commotion near the dungeon caught his eye, and he gazed in horror at all his slaves escaping through the secret passage, protected by his most recent prisoners. Then, he saw Fynballa valiantly fighting three goblins at once.

"That must be her!" he yelled to his guards. "The elf in dark blue armor, near the dungeon. Bring her to me! I shall avenge Gwenore myself!"

Eoin and Fyn fought side by side, slashing, dodging, parrying, and blocking any blade coming their direction. Every now and then, they would glance and grin at each other, wondering how in the world they had gotten themselves into such a series of events in only over a week.

Eoin thought he heard a hobgoblin roar, "Isolate her, sentries!" He then watched in dismay as Fyn became surrounded by five goblins. He rushed to help when an eight-foot guard knocked him out of the way. That guard, backed by another of the same size, struck Fyn in the stomach with his fist, ensuring she wouldn't resist or scream. He then seized her and, carrying her under his arm, rushed away toward the throne room. Eoin lay there, out of breath and deathly scared.

After a few moments of being jostled up unstable stairs, Fyn found herself being tossed toward the throne, where her king sat with his teeth clenched behind his lips.

"Do you know why you are here, child?" he asked.

At first, all Fyn could do was cough and groan.

"Answer me, young fool!"

"I am here," Fyn groaned, "because I murdered your former wife, the queen. I committed a terrible crime against you, and I will face any consequences you give me, just or unjust."

The king, chuckling, stood up and unsheathed his beautiful, yet dirty sword. He sauntered toward her, who was being held by the two hobgoblins. His wide eyes and twitching grimace revealed his full wrath. He now stood in front of her, his sword raised behind his shoulder. After slowly removing her helmet, he purposefully gave a terrible shriek, but before he could budge his sword, Eoin (who had chased after the guards) lunged at him, knocking him over and giving a fighting yell of his own.

"Do not stand idly!" Ever screamed as he wrestled with this intruder. "Kill her, now!"

Just then, one of the guards was shot by a small arrow, and the other's eyes met the reflection of a very bright shield. Ambrose, his doppelgänger, and Ives barged inside and assaulted the second guard, allowing Fyn to crawl toward her weapons, which had been dropped by the first hobgoblin.

The second guard swung its double-sided axe with hard, meticulous throws. Ives, being quite nimble after occasionally dueling cherubim, evaded every swing with ease and found opportunities to slash the beast. Ambrose simply kept out of the axe's range, trying to find a chance to shoot in. Esorbma took a blow to the chest and was launched out the window.

Eoin and Ever rolled back and forth along the carpeted floor, at all costs avoiding each other's blades. When the king saw that Fyn was armed again and attempting to stand, he struggled to break free of Eoin's desperate grip.

Without warning, the entire tower shook violently. The strongest Self-Worthy members had simultaneously thrown some of the rubble at the rook, causing its higher floors to lose their stability and begin to sway. The second hobgoblin lost its balance and tumbled to the floor, where it got pierced once by both of its opponents. Ever had managed to escape Eoin and kicked him away. He trudged to Fyn, who was still on the ground.

"Ever!" Ambrose said in a voice that made the king halt. Ambrose pointed his cutlass at him. "Today, you meet your doom!"

The king just grinned as the second guard got up, still not dead, grabbing Ives and Ambrose from behind and bolting out the window with the two in its grasp. As they fell, the beast yelped and let go of them due to a new arrow wound, and Ives grabbed Ambrose and a second arrow (which looked very much like one of Dilyn's) that stuck into the tower's wall. They were near the ground, so Ives then let go and they dropped.

"We have to get back up there!" Ambrose said the moment he landed.

He and Ives ran to the tower's entrance, but it was blocked by the debris thrown by the other stronger members. Ambrose cursed aloud, looking frantically for another way up while combatting two goblins at once.

A Self-Worthy dwarf ran up to them. "My lord," she said, "the Envoys are here, and they're helping the slaves escape! Shall we pursue them?"

Ives had to kill one more goblin before he could answer. "Nay, let them be. We want the slaves to be freed, and we must occupy ourselves with ridding Ever of his armies. Once the last slave is gone, ensure the Envoys don't follow them, or they will enforce their agenda upon them."

Amory never stopped moving his sword arm; his eyes and his blade constantly darted for any vulnerable area in the armor of his opponents. He didn't have time to glance at his friends who were just as busy, or at the slaves who scurried behind them. Every frantic blow and block by the Envoys paid off, as no one even touched the escapees.

Then, the goblins noticed that there was a gap in the protective line where Fyn and Eoin used to be. A larger goblin acknowledged this to the others, beckoning them to follow it and break through. Edna was the first to see them, as she was next to the gap.

"Guys, over here! There's a hole!"

Nels and Bernice quickly reinforced her. Thankfully the goblins had to go through the thick of the battle, and the Self-Worthy had taken care of quite a few before they could reach the slaves. Bernice charged at them, slid on her knees, and impaled two in one strike. Nels didn't use his arrows this time; he simply wielded his bow like an axe, finding or making chinks in the enemies' armor. Edna smashed any attackers left standing. The three of them stayed there while the others adapted to their larger domains, which were more difficult to keep.

Eventually everyone started to hear thunder. At first, it was faint and easily drowned out by the noises of battle, but the thunderclaps quickly triumphed and could be heard everywhere. Soon, the wall of rain hit, and everyone's job became twice as hard. The fires were gradually put out, but it was almost impossible to see anything, only the occasional shimmer of a blade or a whizzing arrow. The ground was soaked with water and blood of various shades of red, black, and yellow.

"Hurry and escape!" Amory said through the howling wind to those behind him. "We can't protect you much longer!"

The slaves ran as fast as they could without knocking each other over. The Envoys couldn't even see their opponents until they were right on top of them. For Leona and Twyla, this was perfect, but for everyone else, they had to back up again and kill, receiving several wounds in the process.

"Where's Eoin and Fyn?" Nels cried after getting a deep cut in the leg. "We can't hold our positions without them!"

"We'll have to," said Amory, guessing where they might be. Having to dodge another section of wall falling toward him, he got punched in the face by a guard's gauntlet. "I hope they get out of there soon," he groaned to himself as he got back up, his face bleeding in several places.

Ever stood poised to attack, facing the two young elves who had not deteriorated as he had. Eoin and Fyn stood side-by-side, wanting very much just to get out. They and Ever circled each other, the couple subtly inching toward the door.

"She is mine," the king creaked angrily to Eoin. "She must pay for the crime she committed."

Eoin had his teeth clenched and his sword raised. "If you want her, you must get past me first."

"Very well," Ever said as he charged.

Suddenly more debris was thrown, and the top of the tower soon felt the impact. Part of the ceiling above the three elves started leaning toward the courtyard below and finally gave way and fell. Some of the stone blocked the only exit from the throne room, trapping the three on the top, exposed to both rain and arrows. The king quickly ran to a loose section of the wall and ceiling behind him and pulled on it, dodging as it fell, making a blockade on the floor to hinder the Self-Worthy's projectiles. He looked at the couple, who had taken cover behind his throne.

"You have nowhere to turn!" Ever shouted through the rain. "Now, come and face my wrath!"

He leapt behind the throne, trying and failing to hit Fyn. Now that they were out in the open, he lunged at them again, his blade meeting only Eoin's. He shoved Eoin aside and swung at Fyn, but she blocked every strike. Eoin recovered and used his sword to bring Ever's away from Fyn.

"I intend not to kill you," Eoin said, "neither do I mean to let my betrothed die by your hand for any reason."

"Then I shall kill you first!" the king screamed.

The tower continued to rock and the entire castle continued to crumble as Ever rapidly dealt strike after strike. Like the queen, his appearance had diminished, but his skill had not. There was such art and intention with every technique that Eoin and Fyn could not keep up. Eoin was slashed on his arm and hip before Ever knocked him into the barricade of rubble. He then kicked him through the rubble, which made Eoin cry out in pain.

Before the king could finish him off, Fyn pushed Ever away using her shield. He couldn't stop the momentum before she rammed him into the wall. That made his eyes grow wide and hot. He pulled his sword out from between them and started hacking at her, though every hit met her shield. He used his leg to sweep hers from under her, knocking her to the ground. Eoin got up and knocked Ever's sword away again. Ever then found himself between the two elves, fighting them both. He slashed at Eoin, then turned and blocked a blow from Fyn, twisting back and forth with every move made. All three of them also fought for balance as the floor leaned heavily toward the battle below.

Getting tired of this swordfight, Ever cried, "If you will not kill me, then you lose!"

Still, the only hits he received were on his armor. Finally, Fyn smote him in the face with her shield, almost knocking his crown off. That ticked him off enough to grab the shield and swing it, with Fyn holding on, into Eoin. The couple crashed into each other, sending Fyn into the wall of the debris and Eoin through the wall again, finding himself on the edge of the tower. His sword and shield had fallen, and Fyn was too hurt to move. The king jogged to her, sword pointed and eyes blazing. The sword was just shooting down when Eoin dove at Ever once more, and one of them screamed in pain. Fyn sat up and watched Ever stand up from underneath Eoin and pull out his blood-coated blade.

"No!" she cried as she instantly crawled to Eoin, turning him face up. Ever's sword had pierced him just above his breastplate. He had dove straight into the blade. The king stood there, making no sudden moves, waiting to see what would happen next.

Eoin, smiling and coughing up blood, groaned, "You are free now." Then, he lay still.

The mournful cry Fyn uttered could have been heard for several distances. She lay above her fiancé's body, unable to move.

"Now you know how it felt, child," said the king.

"No," said Fyn. "You loved not your wife; you divorced her!"

"This lad said that you were free, thinking my revenge was quenched by his death in your place. Nay, child. I say you both will die!"

Just then, the outer half of the floor fell away from the unstable tower, including where Ever stood. He found himself sliding down the inclined floor, unable to climb back up to Fyn. Before he could grab onto anything, he fell screeching off the tower into the battle below, the falling floor landing after him. Instantly the rain halted, but the thunderous clouds remained overhead as the battle loomed on.

15

THE CURSE AND THE BLESSINGS

S oon after the rain came to a halt, Amory got a chance to take a breath and look around. Though the assault wasn't over, there were not near as many goblins now, only a handful here and there. The castle was mostly filled with the Self-Worthy, who were killing off the remnant of troops loyal to the now-dead king. Ever, his armies, and his reign were forever vanquished.

Only a few slaves were left in the fortress now. Amory called to get their attention. "Go and tell the others to wait for us as we find the other two warriors. We'll come to you soon to help you start your lives again."

"There is no need," said one elf. "We know where to go. If that terrible cry we just heard was from one of those warriors, then you might be delayed in coming anyway. We will be all right. All of our thanks are yours for freeing us from lives of suffering and torment!"

"You're very welcome," said Edna, wiping her brow of sweat and blood. "May Nazir be with you!"

As the last escapees entered the passage and shut the trapdoor, the Envoys went to find a way to Fyn and Eoin. They shifted through the throng of Self-Worthy members, none of them willing to kill each other anymore; they were simply too exhausted to carry the battle on further. The seven of them passed the piece of floor that lay over the king's body. Ambrose and Esorbma were there supervising as others demolished the rubble and began digging the body out. Ambrose's eyes met Amory and Leona's. He gave them a nod and a grateful smile. They only gave kind, slight grins in return. They did not see Dilyn, though they figured he was alive.

Seeing the tower's main entrance was blocked, the Envoys entered a hallway in the roomed wall next to Ever's throne room tower. They rushed to the second floor and entered the tower that way. They ran up the rickety stairs, having to jump a couple of times where some steps were missing. At last, they reached the top but had to pull or smash away more debris before they could get in the throne room.

They burst through, ensuring the room had no goblins or Self-Worthy creatures. They found Fyn lying on Eoin's body. She wasn't standing ready to fight like they thought. She just laid there, stunned, tears rolling from her eyes. She'd barely even looked to see who had entered.

"No, not Eoin!" cried Edna.

"What happened?" Twyla asked.

Between heaving breaths, Fyn answered, "He died in my place. He . . . he dove into the blade that almost slayed me . . . that should have slain *me!*"

Nothing was said for a long while. Everyone sat and joined Fyn in mourning for her love. After a few moments, Fyn said, "There is not much noise outside. Is the battle over? What happened to our king?"

"He's dead," said Neisha. "There were not many goblins left after he fell. And the slaves are all safe and gone."

"Now, I suppose the Self-Worthy will rule Liberdane," Fyn sighed. "Anything would be better than our former king, but I still distrust them." She looked at Eoin's motionless face and began crying again. "I cannot go on without him! Is there nothing that can be done? Is there now no one who can help us . . . who can help me?"

Bernice glanced at her own arm, which used to be infected by a giant spider's venom. "Actually there is one who might be able to help."

Fyn looked up at her companions. "You speak of the Vine, do you not?" She looked back at the body.

"Just give him a try," said Nels.

Fyn sighed deeply, more tears dripping off her chin. "All right."

Leona instantly unsheathed her Dagger and made a green portal. Amory gently lifted the body and carried it through, followed by Fyn and the others. Fyn took one last look at the chaotic remains of Diamond Culet, which was still enveloped in dark clouds, before she stepped through.

Ambrose, flanked by his brother and doppelgänger and covered in battle scars, gazed at Ever's body. Recently unearthed, there was no doubt that he was dead.

Ives limped to Captain Brandt and glanced at the body. "Where is his crown? We cannot secure the kingdom if we do not claim his crown."

One of the jackals who had been digging answered, "It did not fall with him. We pulled the wreckage apart until we reached the dirt and never found it."

"It must still be in the throne room," said Ambrose. "I'm taking most of the armies back to Maewing to inform her that we're ready for her to take Liberdane. Ives, you take a dozen troops and stay here. For one thing, you must find that crown. For another, make sure no one else gets to it first. The Envoys might still want to take Liberdane over in Nazir's name."

"Where are they? Did they leave?" asked Dilyn.

"Yeah, I saw the glow of a portal up in the . . . throne room," said Ambrose.

Ives shouted to a dozen soldiers behind him, "The twelve of you, get up there quickly and ensure they did not take it!" He turned to Captain Brandt. "If they did, we will be here to meet them. If they did not, they will not likely return. I am told that Envoys do not return to a world if their missions in that world are accomplished. Even if they do, it will be too late."

"Are you sure there aren't any goblins left?"

"I am quite certain. Go, and do not worry; worry is always destructive to a soul."

Ambrose called the rest of the armies to the fallen gate, where he summoned a portal from his stolen Sword. As the Self-Worthy departed, Ives waved farewell and turned to go back up the tower where Ever fell. A gleam caught his eye. In a dark corner, he saw the green, glowing eyes of goblins.

"Come back, comrades," he called to his troops, unsheathing his sword. "There are still some enemies alive!"

With the rising sun beginning to pierce through the fading storm clouds, he saw the shimmer of the beasts' menacing blades, along with the intense luster of something else.

"The crown! They have it!"

As she entered the center of the multiverse with the Envoys, Fynballa opened her mouth in awe. Her eyes drank in the white circular portals, the spherical border's nightly look, and the giant Vine in the center with its branches reaching every portal.

"Welcome, Fynballa!" said the Vine in a tone that was more somber, yet still friendly.

"Oh, hello," Fyn replied, surprised to hear the Vine speak. Her superstitions were beginning to wane. "You must be Nazir."

"I am," Nazir said in a way that filled everyone with a sensation of both fear and intrigue. Seeing the body Amory held, he said in a pain-stricken, yet unsurprised voice, "Eoin."

Fyn immediately knelt before him. "Nazir, O King of the multiverse, please, can you bring him back? I do not know if you are even able, but you are my only hope for life anymore."

"You're right," said Nazir, "I am, and have always been, your only hope for life, as well as Eoin's. Yes, I can give his life back, but I must ask you, Fyn: do you believe that I can, and do you accept and believe that I am your ultimate authority, that I can repair the evil caused by you and others to you, and that I am your sole, ever-sufficient source of power, life, and love?"

"Yes," said Fynballa through tears, "I know now that everything these friends of mine said about you was true. I know you reign over everything—the good, the bad, and the painful—and that you will heal the brokenness that I have felt since I was a young child. I accept and believe!"

The Vine "smiled" and chuckled, "Come here, my daughter!" He also called to Amory, "Bring Eoin here."

The Envoys smiled and even cheered as Fyn came close enough for Nazir to embrace her as he had with them. As her mortal blood vapor rose from her body, they couldn't help but feel again what they'd felt when Nazir had redeemed them: freedom, newness, and cleanliness. They also noticed that something else was peeling away from her: the old, ragged garment underneath her armor and newer garment. It tore away in pieces, sliding down her arm and pant sleeves, disintegrating with her former blood.

Then, they noticed that Nazir had placed one of his leaves on Eoin's chest after Amory had set him down. They heard the Vine whisper, "Awaken," and he simultaneously let go of Fyn and the body. The Envoys, now including Fynballa, watched Eoin's lifeless body in angst. They gasped when he budged. Then he slowly inhaled, opened his eyes, looked around, and got up, just as if he had been asleep. Fyn cried even more (this time with a smile like no one had ever seen) and hugged Eoin tightly, and he did the same.

"Yes!" cried both dwarves. Everyone else cheered ecstatically.

After a few long moments, the couple stopped hugging, and Eoin looked around at the Center and at Nazir. He felt for his stab wound; it was merely a flesh wound now. He gazed again at the Great Vine, falling to his knees.

"I . . . I know not what to say! I was just in a place where I was to receive eternal torment; then you brought me back to life! I apologize for every doubtful word I spoke of you. You are indeed everything the Envoys made you out to be!"

"That world you were in is called *Pur*," said the Vine gravely. "That is the only place where I am not; those who are not mine and wish not to have me with them receive that wish after death and forever suffer as a result. That is why it's so important for Envoys to bring me to others, so they won't go there when they die. My Kingdom, which is outside the multiverse yet is flowing into it, is called *Paradeisos*. Only Envoys—my redeemed children—plus my cherubim, are allowed with me there after they die, and eternal paradise is found there because that's where I am."

Nazir continued. "Eoin," he said in a voice that made the elf tremble, "you have long been searching for something, someone, that could fill the void in your life, forgive you of every violation you made of *Integritatem*, and give you purpose and joy. Your king could not, your parents could not, your elderly guardians could not, and Fynballa could not. Do you accept and believe that I am that one who can?"

"Yes, my Lord and my King! I accept and believe."

"Come here, my son!"

More cheering and laughing erupted as the Vine repeated the process with Eoin that he had with Fyn. Eoin had never felt more alive, whole, or loved. When his adoption ended, he rejoined Fyn and held her hand. The Vine then opened a leaf near them and presented their Envoy badges and their new armor molds. They eagerly received them and put on the badges.

"I am proud of you, Eoin!" Nazir exclaimed. "Even though you weren't my child at the time, by giving your life for Fyn, you demonstrated what I had done when I gave my own life for every being, because they, like Fyn, justly deserved to die. Also like you, I came back to life! Henceforth, you will be called Eoin Vyctor, because your love for Fyn, flawed though it was, overcame one of the toughest obstacles known to mortals: the love of self. This is one of the primary traits I want all my Envoys to exhibit. And Fyn, you will soon have the same last name!"

The elves were overjoyed at this news.

"Father," said Amory, "I have a question: I eventually realized that it was wrong to overthrow King Ever, as I said to you in my head last night, but you let the Self-Worthy attack his fortress, and he's dead now. Was it not wrong to go against him, and if so, why did you let the Self-Worthy come?"

"I heard you in your cell last night," the Vine answered, "and I have forgiven you for going against him and the queen and leading the others astray. But yes, it was wrong to go against the king. I appointed Ever and Gwenore, evil though they were. I gave them plenty of chances to turn to me, but they didn't. I let the Self-Worthy assault the king—and you the queen— because they continued to do evil and refused to turn to me. I avenged everyone they exploited, including you five elves and dwarves. I loved the king and queen, but I also love the people they never cared for, and I enforced justice. They were going to face consequences, whether or not you helped. I took vengeance because it was mine to take, and I'm the only one who can rightfully and completely achieve it. However, you did well to free the slaves, for they had toiled under Ever long enough. They constantly cried out for freedom, and I through you finally answered.

"Amory, you along with Eoin and Fyn went against them and let your fury burn against them because you yourselves did not have your parents as authorities over you. Eoin and Fyn, you had your childhood guardians until their time had come, but they were not your parents."

"And I never had anyone as my authority," said Amory. Everyone but Nazir and Bernice was rather surprised to hear this.

"Therefore," Nazir continued, "you showed hostility toward a clear authority who did not use their power well. You didn't know how to treat authorities, so you did what you thought best. That is not an excuse for the choices you made, but I'm exposing this from within you, which you would not have seen by yourselves."

Amory and the elven couple knelt and apologized.

"It is all forgiven. Now, another thing I want to add—and you've already realized this—is that it was also wrong to join the Self-Worthy. I'm not saying that you should stay away from all who are not mine, but they are a movement of their own, seeking to promote their own agenda. They use me and my ideals to support theirs, and some of them match mine, but they will not fully come to me. Marah, my enemy, has deceived them in the shadows, and he deceived you too. Always be watchful of Marah; he will hide and speak behind things that appear just and right but have lies twisted in them. The Self-Worthy is one of those things.

"The Self-Worthy is a political movement. You are not. Envoys are not meant to be political activists. Why? Because my kingdom surpasses politics and worldly affairs. The Envoys' focus is to proclaim my kingdom, not theirs, to those who haven't yet received it, and to train those who do to be Envoys themselves. Do you understand all of this, my children?"

"Yeah," said Bernice. "We're sorry. We didn't know that joining them was that serious. It just sounded like the smart thing to do when we wanted Ever dead."

"You learned much from this mission . . . and no, it's not over yet. Some things you learned the easy way by doing it right the first time, and others you learned the hard way by experiencing the consequences of getting it wrong. But that's where my mercy and providence come in, and I am still glorified by it all. So I want to say to you four humans, who I originally called for this mission, that I'm proud of you, for you did eventually bring me to these two elves, and vice versa, even though you did it the hard way. Honestly though, these two can attest that they wouldn't have come to me unless a tragedy like this occurred."

"It is true," Eoin and Fyn agreed.

"But because they're mine now, I can set things right in Liberdane and reestablish my kingdom there! Ever has no heir to his throne; he and Gwenore had no children. Their family line is all but gone now. The next thing, according to the nation's laws, is that the king's killer takes the throne. However, the king fell from the tower; no one inherently killed him. Therefore, the throne is now open to anyone. In so saying, I myself appoint you, Eoin Vyctor, to be Liberdane's new king, and you, Fynballa, to be their queen. Your wedding will precede your coronation."

"Us?!" the elves cried.

Eoin protested, "But we are not worthy of being rulers of any kind! We do not know all of the laws, let alone how to justly uphold them!"

"If I say you are ready, then you are ready," Nazir said more solemnly. "I did not make a mistake when I chose you, because I led every moment of every event in your lives to prepare you for this calling. You are my Envoys, and if you follow me, you will lead your people well."

The elves were silent, taking all this in. Fynballa had a question she'd wanted answered for decades: "Are you going to lift the Curse of Hertengard, the curse that makes everyone suffer if an evil person rules?"

"No, Fyn, I will not. I initiated it, and I would not call it a curse, because those who make curses wish ill on others, and I do not. It's more of a supernatural punishment, going against what nature previously was. I gave the punishment because Hertengard's forefathers went against me. They confused themselves by thinking good kings were evil, and vice versa, and started treating them backwardly. I altered nature to end the confusion. Earth, the world where the humans live, has a similar punishment, which I also gave after the beginning. I also gave your people *Integritatem*, which showed them explicitly what is good and bad and, most importantly, showed them who I am. I gave this to the humans too, but it has a different name. I am the standard by which a ruler is determined to be good or evil; the difference between a good and bad ruler is the presence or absence of me in their lives.

"Now, Liberdane has gone without a ruler long enough," the Vine continued. "Go into the portal behind me, where a forger and friend will quickly construct your new armor, which is to replace the old. Throw the old apparatus away and put on your new one, which is made to represent me. These Envoys will be waiting here for your return."

Eoin and Fyn paced slowly through the portal, still full of amazement, wholeness, and wonder.

———

"Now, I have more appointments to initiate," Nazir said when the elves were gone. "Neisha. Nels. Twyla. You have served and followed me well. As I've told you in times past, I've never stopped watching and caring for you, even and especially when you yourselves were orphans before you met Ida. Because you've been faithful with little, I will see if you can be faithful with a little more. I am putting you three on Amory's team. You are going to help them change the multiverse!"

"Oh my," said Neisha. "That'd be wonderful!"

"We would be honored!" said Twyla.

"How about that?" Leona said. "The group's growth is picking up speed. We're almost halfway to the 'twenty' Azarias was talking about!"

"Yeah, but we're missing one," sighed Amory. "Nazir, Dilyn never left the Self-Worthy; I think he's going to join them. I'm sorry for causing all this mess! If I hadn't have joined them in the first place . . . ."

"Then he only would've joined them later," the Vine interrupted. "Dilyn loves me, and he loves all of you, but he hasn't let me be King over everything in his life. He still wants to follow his brother because he thinks Ambrose has the final say. Until he becomes disillusioned and realizes I'm the only rightful King, he won't let me guide his decisions. He is still my son, though, and there is much hope that he will return to me, but he won't yet."

———

Eoin and Fyn emerged into the Center again, newly clad in royal-looking armor. They still had the same colors but were more ornate and decorative.

"Those look gorgeous!" said Nels. "You'd better have told Azarias that he outdid himself this time!"

Eoin laughed, "We certainly did compliment him, though he is quite the frightening creature."

"It's true," Nazir added. "You do *not* want to get on his bad side! All right. It's time for you all to return to Liberdane. Eoin and Fyn, you must not be crowned until everything is put right in the land and everyone's needs are fulfilled. The Envoys will help you. Go and joyfully serve your people!"

The nine walked back through the portal out of which they came, excited to finish the mission. Leona, however, turned back just before going through. "Father?"

"Yes, my daughter?"

"Do you want me to tell Dilyn that you miss him? Will telling him something like that help?"

"You can if you want, but I'll tell him myself."

16

MISSIONS: ACCOMPLISHED AND ABOLISHED

The nine Envoys emerged from a newly made portal and found themselves in Diamond Culet's central courtyard. Not much time seemed to have passed. The only difference between now and when they'd left was that the sun had just fully risen, and the Self-Worthy had vanished—and there were some live goblins still standing on the courtyard a few yards away. All of them made eye contact, and the humans began to draw their weapons.

"Wait," said Eoin, stepping forward.

The goblins all raised their arms. "We mean no threat to you," one called.

Edna counted ten troops, then noticed a familiar, luminous object held by one of the stronger goblins.

"You found the crown!" said Fyn.

"We caught it as the king fell," said the first soldier. "This was exactly what that traitor Ives was searching for, but we wanted neither him nor the cult he joined to possess it. He and a few of his minions remained here while the others left, and they tried frantically to seize the crown from us. The score of us who were still alive managed to fight them off, but they slayed half of us in the process. Regrettably all but Ives are dead; he fled for his life, and his whereabouts are unknown. All that to say we would rather crown anyone—as long as he is a loyal, true-blooded elf—than any from that Self-Worthy lot."

Another goblin pointed at Eoin. "You were just dead, were you not?"

"Yes, I was, but the Great Vine Nazir resurrected me. After adopting me as his child, he appointed me to be king of Liberdane and Fynballa to be queen."

"We know not of this Nazir, but we will respect his decision," the second goblin replied. "Our allegiance lies with the king, whoever he might be. Our former king, Ever, is no more, and we are now kingless. We will support you if this is your destiny."

"Do you mean you would follow us loyally?" asked Fyn, surprised.

"Anything is better than the Self-Worthy. Legally we could crown you here and now if you so desire."

Eoin smiled and glanced back at Fyn and the other Envoys. "My thanks are eternally yours, my new friends! However, there is a work of restoration which we must complete first. Lead us to the strategy chamber, and we will discuss plans to revive our long dead land. Only after this will we consent to be crowned."

"And while we're at it," said Amory, "let us tell you more of this Nazir!"

———

Taking short, confident strides, Ambrose approached Maewing's chambers in her fortress in Ourrance. He boldly entered the grand, high-tech room, accompanied only by Dilyn.

In the middle of the white room sat a large, shaded bed adorned with several soft pillows. Amongst the pillows lay Maewing, wearing an ornate white tunic and sitting vertically, her horse legs stretched in front and behind her. She seemed to be recovering abnormally quickly, as her injuries looked less severe, and she'd regained her energy and disposition.

"Captain Brandt, you have returned! What news? Have you conquered Liberdane and seized Ever's crown?"

Ambrose stood tall as he said, "Yes, ma'am! Ever has been vanquished, and Ives is searching for the crown at present as we prepare for you to receive it!"

"You don't currently have the crown?" asked Maewing.

"Well, no," said Ambrose, maintaining his poise. "Ever died by falling, and we don't know exactly where the crown is, but I assure you that Ives and his team will recover it."

Maewing was appalled. "His team? Does that mean the rest of our armies returned with you?! Ambrose, why did you come back? Ives and a dozen troops are not enough to secure a kingdom! With Diamond Culet left vulnerable, anyone could take the crown!"

"But there's no one else there!" shouted Ambrose, forgetting his manners. "All the goblins are dead; the castle's virtually empty if not for Ives! We still have a secure hold on Liberdane!"

Just then, Lisias, fully recovered from his injuries, burst through the door panting, "Your majesty, I have just come from Diamond Culet. In hiding, I saw almost a dozen remaining goblins in the courtyard in possession of the crown, and they have bestowed it upon another young elf who was flanked by Envoys!"

Maewing sat there, making no movement. "And Ives?"

"There is no trace of him, your highness."

Maewing slowly turned her gaze toward Ambrose, who stood pale and motionless. Dilyn rethought his assumptions on the Self-Worthy's friendliness.

Maewing uttered coolly, "It matters little whether you were lying or if something drastic happened between now and your departure from the castle. The fact is that we have lost our chance to seize and free Hertengard." She let that sink in for a few moments. "Ambrose, I would have been fine with you being king of Liberdane yourself because of the strong leader I thought you were. Now, I know better. I hereby immediately demote you to the rank of a common soldier until you learn to lead properly. You may keep your cutlass and crossbow, but I must have your shield—and the Sword of *Chârâsh*."

"I thought you said I could keep it," said Ambrose, regaining his wits. "Am I now not *worthy* to have it, because I think I am worthy by my own right."

"Your actions have proven otherwise," said Maewing, trying very hard not to lose her temper. "You are not dependable with such a treasure. Since I have a thorough knowledge of it, that Sword shall now be mine."

Ambrose sauntered to Maewing's bed, intention and anger in his every step. As he handed the Sword in its sheath to his commander, he whispered, "Is this what you were getting at all along?"

Maewing ignored the question and looked up at Dilyn, her expression changing almost completely to one of welcoming kindness. "Who is this you have brought with you?"

"I . . . I'm Dilyn, Ambrose's brother. I wanted to join you and your armies."

Maewing grinned. "And what made you make this decision, my friend?"

"I want to make a real difference. I want to feel like I mean something and that my life can contribute to the betterment of the multiverse. I feel like the Self-Worthy is the best way to do that; the Envoys don't offer much protection and fulfillment as far as I can see."

"Yes," Maewing sighed, "perhaps the rumors are true that Nazir makes many promises but fails to accomplish them. Welcome to the Self-Worthy, Dilyn! You are now on the path of self-realization and fulfillment! I look forward to you joining our ranks."

Lisias cheered and shook Dilyn's hand. Ambrose let go of his anger enough to grin and pat his brother on the back.

"One question," said Dilyn. "Do I need to have my Envoy armor and bow replaced, or can I remain in both groups?"

"Oh, no, you can keep them!" Maewing said. "We have plenty of Envoys and former Envoys in our comradery. Take Lisias here, for example. He forsook the Vine long ago, yet he still wears the armor he gave him. Joining the Self-Worthy does not replace any part of who you are—it adds to it!"

Maewing then turned to Lisias. "Call everyone together and proclaim this message on my behalf: Hertengard is lost for now. The former Captain Brandt has returned empty-handed. It has come to my attention that wholescale assaults are necessary and critical to free each realm. It will be a long while before this can happen, however, as we require physical and emotional recovery, plus many more volunteers." Then, she said to herself, *This dream is costing more time than I originally planned.*

"Consider it done, my lady," bowed Lisias, and he exited her chambers with Ambrose and Dilyn.

On their way to the courtyard, Dilyn whispered to Ambrose, "So that's the leader of the Self-Worthy?"

"Yeah," mumbled Ambrose. "She's a legendary warrior and commander, but her mood changes on a whim, and it's hard to tell what she'll say or do."

"You still think it was worth it to join these guys?"

Ambrose sighed deeply. "For now. I thought I would climb to the top of the ladder of ranks more quickly, but I just got demoted. At one moment, I go from private to captain, and the next moment, I'm back to private. I'm committed to this now, though; there's no turning back."

Dilyn thought Ambrose was wrong but said nothing.

It had been four months since Eoin and Fynballa had become Envoys, and they had been busy each day since. Before they began restoring the land and the people's livelihoods, they first gave King Ever a proper elven burial, something they wished they could do for Queen Gwenore. Eoin placed the body in the wooden casket, as it was customary for the king's successor to do. The ceremony was held at sunset on the very day the nine Envoys returned from the Center. Not many showed up for the funeral, but the Envoys made it special and traditional nonetheless.

Each day afterward was spent in the villages and farms, where Eoin and Fyn, along with the others, tilled land, prepared meals and clothing, and repaired homes, businesses, tools, and families. While performing each task (all with a smile), they told their people about Nazir and managed to bring many to him. Among these were the guards who had protected the crown. When Nazir redeemed them, they morphed from goblins back to noble elves. These would become Eoin and Fyn's most trusted and courageous soldiers.

As they went from town to town, the Envoys noticed that the land was changing. The grass turned from blond to deep green, the tree trunks regained their color, and the storm clouds became less frequent and more profitable for the land, which was much more fertile. Vegetables began to grow again, and the livestock were quickly fattened by the luscious grass. The trees themselves grew clear, crystalline leaves, glistening as they would in a sunrise after an overnight freeze. Some even produced fruit and flowers with the appearance of gems, just as Fynballa had described.

By the time their help reached everywhere in Liberdane, the land looked entirely different, as if it had been created afresh. Eoin and Fyn reported this to Nazir after every individual had been helped, and Nazir said it was now time for them to be wed and crowned. It was at this point that they repaired Diamond Culet. This proved to be quite simple; all Ever's additions for fortification were destroyed when the Self-Worthy attacked, so all that needed to be done was cleaning the rubble and rearranging several items, namely the thrones. The goblins-turned-elves said the thrones were meant to be on the back wall in the courtyard so the rulers could easily be accessed by the people. Ever had put them in the towers so he wouldn't be killed as easily.

When Diamond Culet was finally restored and decorated for the ceremony, Eoin and Fyn prepared for their new roles as spouses and leaders after the four months of renewal. Amory and his team were placed by Nazir as guards for the event, though they could still watch every moment of it.

The ceremony was held in the courtyard, whose walls were adorned with the gemlike leaves and flowers, as well as banners and flags with Liberdane's colors: crimson to signify the land's history, indigo to represent the present prosperity, and gold to resemble future hope. There were also golden banners with the Envoys' emblem, including Bernice's flag, which she held high. Each Envoy took his or her position at one of the five towers, with Bernice joining Amory and Nels joining his sister, all four of whom were at the back towers near the thrones. In the courtyard itself stood many elven and dwarfish villagers and converted soldiers, lords, and ladies. In front of the thrones at the back wall stood the one honorable minister who had been enslaved for so long, back in his white gown and golden wreath.

Trumpets suddenly sounded, and everyone turned to see Eoin walking stately from the front tower down an aisle made by the crowd. His beard had been trimmed up to his chin, and his straight hair was cut to his shoulders, something that hadn't been done in years. Along with a beaming smile, he wore a velvet uniform with a golden cape and brown boots. He came and stood before the minister, then turned around when the trumps blew again. From the front tower now came Fynballa with an even more radiant smile than Eoin's. Her hair she kept uncut and unbound, falling to her feet behind her. She wore a white, flowing dress with tints of blue and brown sandals inlaid with sapphire, plus blue flower jewels intertwined in her hair. Some had marveled over Eoin's might and Fyn's beauty in the past decades, but gazing at them now astounded everyone beyond words.

When Fyn joined Eoin at the front, the minister began the wedding. He had them recite vows like those human spouses make (though Eoin and Fyn were made to memorize them rather than repeating the minister). However, there were some unique vows of which Bernice took note.

"I swear," said Eoin, "to protect and lead our family, our kingdom, and especially you to the utmost—whether or not you are able to protect yourself—even and especially if that means abandoning my life again so that you will keep yours for centuries to come until the Vine calls me home."

"I swear," said Fynballa, "to fight for our union, our descendants and legacy, and our kingdom to the utmost as you do the same, even if that means abandoning my life so that our legacy and our nation will remain for millennia to come until the Vine calls me home."

"I swear," Eoin declared, "to raise and provide for our children, as long as the Vine grants this, according to *Integritatem*, so that our legacy might be one that points all to the one who founded *Integritatem*."

"I swear," Fyn added, "to raise and teach our children, as long as the Vine grants this, according to *Integritatem*, so that our legacy might be one that points all to the one who founded *Integritatem*."

At that, they were granted permission to kiss and were finally wed after decades of waiting and running. As they applauded with the crowd, Amory and Bernice glanced at each other and grinned as they had never done before. The minister immediately began the coronation by asking both Eoin and Fyn to recite one more vow together.

"We swear as Envoys of the Vine to follow our divine King and to lead lives that would represent him: in our union, our family, and our kingdom of Liberdane. We swear to lead the nation into battle only if necessary and to follow the nation into peace. We swear to make actions and decisions that benefit the people more or rather than ourselves, until the Vine calls us home, leaving Liberdane more prosperous, peaceful, and aligned with the Vine than when we were born."

The minister then turned to take the crowns sitting on the thrones behind him. He took the queen's first, which had been recovered from the ruins of Gwenore's castle (none from the Self-Worthy had thought to search for it). This crown was almost identical to the king's; it was made of transparent diamond and gold and had long, thin wings on either side. After crowning Fynballa, he laid the king's crown—now completely clean—on Eoin's brow.

The minister had the couple turn to the people, holding hands in the air. He professed, "It is with great joy and honor that I bestow upon you King Eoin Vyctor and Queen Fynballa Vyctor of Liberdane! May your reign be long and far greater than that of your predecessors!"

The crowd, along with the Envoys, gave cheers that had not been heard nor given in Liberdane in almost a century. Eoin and Fyn laughed with excitement, inwardly thanking Nazir for giving all of this to them.

Eoin looked back at Amory and Bernice. Through the applause Amory shouted, "I only wish Nazir were actually here!"

"I believe he is!" said Eoin, looking at something behind them. Amory and Bernice turned to see a small cluster of vine branches sprouting along the side of the wall.

Bernice chuckled. "We can't escape him even if we tried!"

Thus commenced the legendary reign of Eoin and Fynballa Vyctor. Liberdane, along with all Hertengard, benefitted immensely under their leadership for centuries. The food and treasures that came from Liberdane far exceeded the worth of the other nations'. The people, elves and dwarves alike, had become strong, joyful, and united, especially the orphans and others with misfortunes. Eoin was mighty and strong in his rule, and his subjects and rivals admired and feared him. And in all Liberdane, there was no one fairer than Fynballa, neither in justice nor in beauty.

Amory stepped into the study in his colonial home in Philadelphia. He opened his laptop and launched his video conference app. Within minutes, Bernice, Leona, and Edna joined the conference.

"Hello, all!" Amory began. "How's everyone doing?"

"Doing well, thanks," said Leona. "Life's starting to get back to normal. By the way, congrats on your graduations, Amory and Bernice!"

"Thanks!" Bernice said. "It was a bit of a struggle since we were in another world for a whole semester, but we finally finished! Those summer classes we took, along with completing the last midterms early, really paid off. Edna, you're the one in the home stretch now!"

"Yeah," Edna sighed, "and it's more stressful than ever."

"Oh, you've got this!" Leona said. "If I can do it, you certainly can! So, Amory, how are our new team members?"

"I visited them last week, and they're doing great! Nels and Neisha are currently serving as Eoin and Fyn's advisors, since Eoin and Fyn are still new Envoys. Twyla's back at Ida's orphanage, making sure they're well taken care of before Twyla resigns. They all seem to be quite excited about working with us."

"I can say the same about them!" said Edna. "So, you graduates, what are you going to do now?"

"I quit my job as a waitress," Bernice said. "I'm trying to get a job in HR, which is what I got my bachelor's in. No results yet."

"I've still got my job apprenticing under a mechanic," Amory put in. "That's doing well for me—enough for me to court Bernice!"

"*What?!*" Leona gasped with excitement. "*Since when?*"

"Two weeks ago," Bernice said. "We've been on a couple dates so far, and it's been good!"

"Nazir thinks it's a good idea, so I jumped at the chance!" Amory chuckled. "We've now got a king and queen who are good role models for us. What about you, Leona? How's life in Stonesboro?"

"It's going well. That job I got as a teacher at Dilyn's school a couple months ago is tough, but it's what I enjoy . . . I teach better than I learn. I wear my armor there every day, and I frequently get asked by my students about it, so I get to tell them about Nazir!"

"Yeah," Edna added, "I've been wearing my armor more often now, and I sometimes get to do the same thing. It's awkward at times, but I'm getting used to it."

"How is Dilyn?" Amory asked.

"He seems happy," said Leona. "I get to teach one of the classes he's in, and he always chats with me after it's over. Apparently he's quite enthusiastic about both Nazir and the Self-Worthy since he raves about his visits to both. I've seen him talk to others about how wonderful the Self-Worthy is, while I've been talking to the same ones about the Envoys, so there's a bit of pressure there. On the outside, he's happy; on the inside, I sense some confusion still eating at him. It may take time for that to surface, though. Part of that probably has to do with Ambrose leaving for Yale; he's still very passionate about this group and manages to win several to their cause. I keep asking Nazir to open their eyes and awaken them from this illusion, and he says he gradually is, but it's still hard to see them like this."

"Yeah," Amory sighed, "let's all keep asking Nazir to do this. He's the only one who can do anything for them now. In the meantime, keep up the training and visiting him. We now know it literally does a world of good! We'll see you later!"

"See ya!" said Leona and Edna, and they logged off, leaving Amory and Bernice alone.

"Who'd have thought that all this would've happened within a year?" Bernice said.

"Only one!" Amory exclaimed.

"You know, I'm glad he appointed you as our leader. I don't think anyone could've done better."

"You wouldn't have said that last year, seeing how immature I was before him. And I'm not just saying this because you complimented me, but I'm overjoyed to have you learning and fighting by my side. I can't imagine anyone else in your place."

Bernice grinned. "My thanks are yours!"

After saying their goodbyes, Bernice logged off. Amory sat back in his cushioned chair, smiling. "And my thanks are forever yours, Father!"

At that, he shut the laptop, waited a moment, and unsheathed his Dagger.